MY KIND OF FASHION MODEL

BIG 4 TRUCKING #2

VICTORIA STAAT

MY KIND OF FASHION MODEL
Copyright © 2018 by Victoria Staat

ISBN: 978-1-68046-575-4

Published by Satin Romance
An Imprint of Melange Books, LLC
White Bear Lake, MN 55110
www.satinromance.com

Names, characters, and incidents depicted in this book are products of the author's imagination or are used fictitiously. Any resemblance to actual events, locales, organizations, or persons, living or dead, is entirely coincidental and beyond the intent of the author or the publisher. No part of this book may be reproduced or transmitted in any form or by any means, electronic or mechanical, including photocopying, recording, or by any information storage and retrieval system, without permission in writing from the publisher except for the use of brief quotations in a book review or scholarly journal.

Published in the United States of America.

Cover Design by Fantasia Frog Designs

1

Jimmy, the Big 4 Trucking mechanic straddled the middle of a big rig motor, trying to loosen bolts off a valve cover with his impact wrench. He'd only gotten two screws out of the greasy engine head. When exhaustion came over him.

He leaned back against the firewall of the truck and wiped the perspiration from his brow. Seemed as though the days were never long enough. There was always an endless line of big rigs that needed repairs, and damn he was tired.

His girlfriend, Tina, wasn't any help either with her constant need to have him right there with her, every moment he wasn't working.

Jimmy took a deep breath. Because with her, it was always about going to the bar and doing the nasty all night long. He never thought he'd ever think bars and sex with a good looking woman would get old. But, as God as his witness, it sure the hell had.

On top of all that, there was the run every morning from her apartment to his house, where he changed and headed for work. Hell, if it wasn't for that, he'd never have any time to himself.

Jimmy thought he was a fairly intelligent man. He even tried to be a good guy, especially with women. He ran his fingers through his short brown hair as he tried to figure this whole mess out.

Hell, he didn't know how he got into this relationship with Tina in the first place. Then a light bulb went on in his head. He knew exactly why; it was all about the sex. Boy, was she great at it. It was like she took classes on how to please a man. Jimmy found he wasn't willing to give that up, at least not yet. He sighed at the thought.

However, Jimmy realized he had to do something about his crazy life style. But hell, whenever he brought up the idea of taking a day or two for himself. Tina turned on the water works. Man, he hated when she cried so he ended up giving in to her. Damn it to hell, what was he going to do? This wild pace he was living was really paying a toll on him.

Again, weakness surged through his body, and he could hardly keep his eyes open. At that moment he knew he had to get some much needed sleep, or he was going to fall asleep right there on the engine. So with a deep breath, he headed for the office and a big cup of strong, black, energy —coffee.

He had just poured a large cup of coffee, when he noticed his partners were staring out the full glass office door. They seemed to be fixated on something out in the truck yard, so he went over and looked out the door too.

There he stood staring at his other partner—Trent.

Jimmy tried to get closer. He wanted to hear what Trent was yelling at his new wife, Candy, about. However, it seemed as though he couldn't catch the gist of the whole conversation. Damn, they were too far away. So, Jimmy and his two other partners, Bobby and Benet, tried to eavesdrop.

While they stared out the window, Jimmy recalled how Candy and Trent fell in love. It was nearly one year ago. A trucker and a bar owner hit it off quickly, after Candy beat him up one night in her bar. He smiled at the thought.

The couple struggled through secrets, mystery and deceit to be together. And here a year later, they stood in the middle of the truck yard arguing. He couldn't help but wonder what set this off.

He couldn't imagine what was going on? The couple had only been married a year, and after a few months of training, Candy had earned her CDL License; she wanted to drive trucks. Jimmy was amused because she loved to drive and was pretty darn good at it too. She was proving to be a great asset to Big 4 Trucking. Most importantly, he thought the two of them had been getting along beautifully. Until now, that is.

There was no doubt in Jimmy's mind they would make up. But, at this point Candy had her hands on her hips and was yelling at Trent. Not only did they have Jimmy's full attention, there was also dead silence from Benet and Bobby. Until a smile came to Jimmy slowly. At that moment he watched as Trent pulled a crying Candy into his arms and hugged her. His wife's head rested on his chest. Jimmy thought it was a touching scene. Boy, was he a sucker for a happy ending.

In that instant, he knew what he wanted; what Trent and Candy had. A relationship which could breach any argument, or problem. Yeah, he wanted, love. He just wasn't sure Tina was the one, though.

Seven miles away, Kelsey Curtis stood in front of her bedroom mirror. Big, bright green eyes sparkled back at her, and she couldn't help but smile.

Today she was happy. Seemed as though she hadn't felt this good in years. She attributed her good spirits to the little town she had just moved to. There was something different about Port Austin. It had her thinking this was finally the time to build a life for herself, right here in this quaint little place.

Maybe she'd even find a man? Her hands traced over her feminine curves. She wondered where that came from? No sooner had the thought crossed her mind and she understood.

It had been an awfully long time since she'd been with a man, been held, kissed, or even touched. Suddenly a particular man crossed her mind. He was a guy who came into one of the bars she worked at.

The truth was, she took a liking to him; he took a liking to her. They were like ships passing in the night. They found comfort in each other's arms for the evening, and then he'd leave.

Kelsey took a deep breath, leaned in close to the mirror and looked right into her own eyes. Heaven help her, the memory of his caress was warm and inviting and the thought sent a lonely shiver through her body.

With closed eyes she remembered him. Guess she would always have a soft spot for her first. Yes, he was the one who'd made her heart tremble and her body ache for the first time in her life. Although, that was all there was between them, and she wanted so much more.

A deep breath escaped her lungs as she stood straight up. Seemed as though she was always so busy protecting herself from being found, men became off limits for her.

However, now things were different. She'd been running for nearly six years. Yes, six years of fear and worry was finally behind her. Only a bright future lay before her. Kelsey was positive Port Austin would be her fresh new start, and maybe, just maybe she'd find a nice man too. The idea of letting down her guard, meeting a man and building a new life sounded a bit scary, but wonderful all at the same time.

Kelsey took a black tube of mascara off the dresser under the mirror, and began brushing her eyelashes in the mirror, as she thought about a family and children. Heaven help her, she couldn't believe she was even thinking about kids. Oh my God, little ones were always considered taboo in her mind. Kelsey wouldn't allow herself to go there, because the idea of being on the run and never having them, broke her heart. So she always put it out of mind. It was less painful that way.

She placed the mascara back on the dresser, picked up a tube of lipstick, and slid it over her lips as she wondered why this town made her happy, and gave her new hope? Kelsey rubbed her lips together to blend in the color, and smiled into the mirror.

It had to be because it was time. It had been six long, worried years since she'd seen the monster. She believed he'd forgotten her, or at least didn't know where she was. Either way, she was free; free to start a life of her own.

Kelsey placed her hands on her hips. Grinned at her own special look in the mirror and said, "Now's the time to start your new life."

She lifted the classified newspaper off her freshly made bed and showed it to herself in the mirror. "Okay, Kelsey, all you need is to find a job, and make a life for yourself, so get going."

Back at Big 4 Trucking, Jimmy was still looking out the door with his partners. The argument between Trent and Candy was over, and he was glad they seemed to have made up.

"Well, whatever it was they fought about seems to be patched up now," Jimmy announced to his partners.

He saw his partners nod. Truth was he knew they were all glad the matter was straightened out. Because Trent and Candy meant a lot to all of them.

"Hey Bobby, have you found us a new dispatcher yet?" Benet asked in his deep baritone voice.

"Man, I must have interviewed a hundred people; men and women. Not a one of them would fit the job, or the money isn't good enough. Even Jimmy here seems to be a problem." Bobby took a deep breath.

Jimmy jumped to his own defense. "Hey, what do you mean by that, Bobby?"

"Let's face it, once you're under the hood of a truck, you're oblivious to the rest of the world."

"Oh, c'mon, I said hi to the last woman you introduced me to."

"No, Jimmy, you grunted, big difference!" Bobby shook his head at the youngest partner.

"What do you want from me? I'm not Mr. Personality like you are. I have so much work, I should be four people."

Clearly, the expression on Benet's face changed, right before Jimmy's eyes. There was no doubt he was holding something back. He knew Benet was always a good humored guy. Hell, he also remembered Benet even grinned when he punched someone in the mouth. Yet today it looked as though something was eating away at his big partner. His great disposition seemed to have soured. Jimmy sure didn't understand it.

However, a moment later he found out exactly what was on his partner's mind. Because next he watched Benet leaf through his mail as he said nonchalantly, "If you weren't out all night, every night, with that little Hoochi Mamma of yours, you'd have a little energy for your job."

Jimmy stood completely still for a split second while what Benet said sunk in. Then he took what he thought was a threatening step toward his partner with anger in his eyes. And when Benet grinned at him, steam seemed to come out of Jimmy's ears. But, before he could start a fight with Benet, Bobby jumped in between the two of them.

Jimmy's face went bright red with rage. All Benet did was grin at him. However, Bobby never let loose of his grip on Jimmy's shoulders.

"Do you really want to come to blows with Benet? Look at the man. He's a damn mountain for crissakes. You want to risk your life for a woman?" Bobby warned.

"Yeah, Jimmy, do you?" Benet said, just to egg on his youngest partner.

Now Jimmy knew, Benet was the biggest of all four partners. Six foot, eight and two hundred and seventy five pounds of pure muscle. Curly brown hair filled his head and spilled over onto his forehead. Deep brown eyes and a broad smile made him a heart breaker to all the women.

However, their mechanic also understood men knew by Benet's size alone, he could break you in half if he had the inclination, yet he bent over backward to end things peacefully. Still, Jimmy realized early on, he wasn't a guy to tangle with.

Yet, when Jimmy watched the mountain of a man found the situation humorous, he tried to get to Benet. He knew he should be worried, but damn, he was tired as hell, and just plain pissed. So thank God Bobby stepped between them again at that moment.

"Don't even think about fighting with Benet. Just go back into the garage and take it out on a motor, or something," Bobby suggested.

Jimmy gave Benet a dirty look because the wide aggravating grin was still on his face. So he stormed out of the office and into the garage with a slam of the door.

Benet couldn't hold back his big booming laugh at the thought of Jimmy trying to pick a fight with him. The whole thing was ridiculous.

"Why in the hell did you have to say that crap to Jimmy? You made a rule in the very beginning, remember, Benet? The rule was not to let women get between partners. Our women are our own personal problem, and now you go and say something like that Hoochi Mamma remark to the kid," Bobby said as he shook his head at his partner.

Benet sat on the edge of Bobby's desk, his mail still in his hand. The truth was he couldn't hold back the nagging worry he had about their youngest partner, who he liked to call the Kid.

He was remembering the night Jimmy met his girlfriend. He happened to be with him at the bar and grill. She hung on the kid, wouldn't let him out of her sight. However, when Jimmy went to the rest room, she turned her attention to him. Benet shook his head, because she had propositioned him right there at the bar.

Man, that woman had loose morals. He walked away that night, but

Jimmy didn't. And now the kid was tangled in her web. So he had to spill out what he thought was a fact. "She is a Hoochi Mamma," Benet insisted.

"Will you stop calling her that?"

"Well, she is, and Jimmy's not a kid anymore. You know as well as I do, Bobby, the girl has her claws in him deep. And he's eating up all the sex she's giving him with a spoon."

"So what if it's true, Benet? We have no right sticking our nose in his business."

"It is our business when Jimmy's too tired to get his work done. Because if he's not exhausted from doing her all night he's waiting for her to call like a love sick puppy dog, and I haven't even gotten to the age difference."

How much older do you think she is?" Bobby's curiosity was peaked.

Hell, ten years, if not more.

Benet watched Bobby as he slowly leaned back on the counter across from him. He could tell by the expression on his partner's face, he was shocked by the age difference.

"Whether we like it or not, Benet, it happens," Bobby admitted with a shrug.

"Maybe so, but do you think Jimmy's up for what she can put him through? Not me. The woman will have everything he's got in less than six months, and we'll be scraping poor Jimmy off the floor. And, give this some thought, Bobby. Do you want the bitch as a partner? Because if she gets him to marry her, she can get half of everything in the divorce. That means she'll have half of his share in Big 4 Trucking."

One look at Bobby still deep in thought and Benet knew he'd made his point. He finally put his worry out there. The kid was playing with fire and at this point Benet was worried sick, it could start a fire that could take all of them with him.

So with that in mind, Benet said, "I've got to make this delivery, I'll be back later."

Benet walked out of the office, jumped into his truck and took off with his load. Leaving Bobby to consider all the ramifications of Jimmy's relationship.

An hour later, Bobby sat at his desk leafing through a stack of applications for dispatchers. He was preparing for some interviews in the afternoon.

However, he was having a heck of a time concentrating. It seemed as though he couldn't get what Benet said, out of his mind. Bobby tried not to get involved in his partner's personal life. But hell, Jimmy's romance with this woman could cause a huge problem for Big 4.

A moment later, Bobby was pulled from his thoughts because Trent walked in and sat down in the chair right in front of his desk. Bobby hoped the smile on his face, was a clue the couple had made up. So he grinned back at him.

"We all saw you and Candy arguing. Do you want to talk?" Bobby asked.

"No, it's just pretty cut and dry. Candy's pregnant," Trent said as a matter of fact.

The smile on Bobby's face grew quickly, and he came around the desk and gave his partner a one armed hug. "Congrats, Trent," he said as he leaned back against the desk, his arms folded across his chest. "You a father, yeah, I can see that. Although, I'm sure the kid will be making his own bed at age three, seeing you're such a neat nick. Bobby chuckled. "So, what were you two arguing about?"

"The baby," Trent answered the question.

"I don't understand."

"Look, Bobby, when we were first married we agreed to wait two years for children. It has only been a year and we're only just starting to see a nice profit here at Big 4. It's just bad timing."

"You don't still feel that way, do you?" Bobby was taken aback.

"Do I still think its bad timing? Yes. Do I want our baby? Hell, yeah! Just never the easy way."

"Yeah, Trent, I know."

"Oh, I didn't get a chance to talk to you earlier. How's the hunt for a dispatcher going?"

"Not good, I'm beginning to think it would be easier to find another trucker, or salesman, than a dispatcher. And I just had to defuse a problem earlier between Jimmy and Benet." Bobby shook his head.

"What the hell happened? "Trent seemed surprised.

"Benet's a little ticked off about Jimmy's work lately. Although I think the real reason is, he hates his girlfriend. He's worried about Jimmy and what this woman could do to him. And, if she did get Jimmy to marry her, it wouldn't be long before they would be divorced, which would leave her with a big share in Big 4. Hey, what is a Hoochi Mamma?" Bobby switched topics quickly.

"Why?" Trent chuckled.

"Because Benet called Jimmy's girlfriend a Hoochi Mamma. You know Benet, he's so blasé about everything, it's hard to say. But, on a scale from one to ten, I would say he was an eleven."

"Well, Bobby, I don't think we've heard the end of this. When Benet gets something in his craw, he hangs on like a bulldog." Trent shrugged. "It's a woman with no morals, one who dresses and looks just like a bit of a floozy, to say it nicely."

Bobby gave him a strange look.

"That's what a Hoochi Mamma is," Trent explained.

All Bobby did was laugh.

Seven miles away, Kelsey stood sipping a cup of coffee. She was blowing on it to cool it down. It wasn't long before her java was just right.

With another sip of the caramel colored liquid, she looked out over her new lower flat. Thank God the place was furnished because now she was staring at eight cardboard boxes stacked in the middle of the living room. Only a portable sewing machine sat next to the pile of cartons.

Here she was, twenty four years old and her entire life could fit into those cardboard squares, and her used sewing machine was her only cherished item. Yet she still had a warm feeling in her chest about this place. Even now it felt like home.

A deep breath escaped her lungs. She was healthy, happy and in charge of her own life. At this point she was glad to finally feel safe.

Port Austin was a sweet, little, old fashioned town— just the kind of place she'd been looking for. She was done running. Her heart swelled with hope and excitement that this place would be her new forever home.

She drank down the very last drop of coffee and placed her empty coffee cup in the sink. Then she took her black blazer off the chair and slid her arms into the sleeves. Smoothed down the collar, and fluffed her hair up just a little.

And with a smile on her face, she said, "Okay, Kelsey, it's time to find your destiny."

She slung her sack purse over her shoulder. And with the classified section of the newspaper under her arm, she headed out into the world.

2

Bobby sat at his desk, surrounded by stacks of applications, resumes included. To be honest, he didn't know if he'd ever see his desk again. Hell, he felt like if he interviewed one more person, he would lose his mind. Yes, the hours were long, but for god sakes, there had to be someone who could work with them.

At this point, he tried to think of a way to encourage people to want the long hours and the low salary. But hell, they couldn't offer more money, especially without seeing how they work. And, the job was what it was. He couldn't change that. So he took a deep, calming breath and went back to looking through the stack of applications.

A moment later, the full glass door of Big 4 Trucking opened and in walked a young woman. She stood about five foot four, and her hair was the first thing Bobby noticed because it was very short and spiked all over her head. It was also frosted heavily with white streaks. Silver crosses dangled from her ears, and a larger thick, intricate filigree cross hung around her neck. She wore black snug pants, a white collared shirt covered with a black blazer.

Bobby looked up from the tip of the chunky black shoes on her feet, to the top of her short spiked hair. Then took another deep breath as he thought, *here we go again*.

"Can I help you?" Bobby said in a very business-like manner.

"I hope so. I'm here about the job," she said with confidence.

He leaned back in his chair and looked up at her. "Do you have a resume?"

"No, I don't have a resume, but could I please fill out an application?" She seemed eager.

He snatched an application from the desk drawer. And watched her as she sat in a chair on the other side of his desk filling out the white paper form.

"What kind of experience do you have?" Bobby questioned.

While she filled out the application, he noticed her black fingernail polish.

"I've done a lot of reception work. I've even dispatched cabs in the city," she told him.

"Detroit?"

"Yes, I lived there most of my life," she replied.

"How do you feel about working for four men? Because that's what Big 4 is all about, four truckers trying to make a living. Do you think you can handle four surly guys all at the same time?"

He saw her put the pen down and look up at him. "Sir…" she began.

"My name is Bobby Weston, everyone just calls me plain, Bobby."

"Alright, Bobby, I have worked with lots of guys, in a cab company and in bars. Believe me, if I can handle those guys, I can work for four men,"

"Do you think you can be a trucking dispatcher, here in our office and garage? Because this is where Big 4 operates. I call in sales jobs from the road. The other guys may need to know about runs, changes in loads, even unexpected pick ups. Any one of us at any time could call in with a mechanical question for Jimmy."

"Who's Jimmy?" she asked.

"Our mechanic and partner. He's important to all three of us. Jimmy keeps our trucks running. He's the guy who helps us stay on the road. You'll be working closely with him, all the time. The job pays $450.00 a week, that's salary, but I have to warn you. The hours are long, and we'll want you to totally take care of the office while we're gone,"

"Sir, are you making this all up? If I didn't know better, I'd swear you're trying to talk me out of this job." She looked horrified.

Bobby chuckled. "Yeah, I know, this is where I lose all of my applicants, still I want to be perfectly honest with you. This job will turn into a career. Big 4 needs someone who is willing to give it their all. The question here is are you willing to do that? Because we need someone we can trust, someone with whom we can all get along. If you're not the one, you'll have to excuse me if I go back to looking through these resumes."

Bobby stared at her as he waited calmly for her to pick up her purse and run for the hills because none of the other applicants had even gotten this far. However, to his surprise, she sat there staring back at him, until a moment later when she broke the silence.

"My name is Kelsey Curtis. I'm twenty-four years old, and I've done a bunch of different jobs."

His eyes widened when she leaned across the desk and said as a matter of fact, "I'm not a weakling who can't take care of herself. I'm tough, I get along very well with men, and I'm excellent on the radio."

"So, am I to take it, you want the job?" Bobby held his breath.

"Yes, Sir, I do want the job. I need the work and the money. I'll work hard for you, and after a while, I promise you this office will run like a well oiled machine. You'll see, and I learn fast." She nodded for emphasis.

Bobby sat back deeply into his leather chair and rocked back and forth grinning at her. Yet all that came out of his mouth was, "So, you're a little Goth girl?"

"Yes, Sir, Mr. Weston, but if it offends you, I'll change my look."

Bobby leaned across the desk and smiled at her. "It doesn't offend me, nor do I think my partners will mind. As long as you don't bite any chicken's head off, you'll get no complaints from us. Just remember, we do get clients in here, so if you dress like you are right now, I have no complaints."

"Am I hired then?" She seemed excited.

"Yes, Kelsey Curtis, you have the job. In fact, can you start today?"

"Yes, Sir!" she blurted out.

"Kelsey, stop with the Sir thing, I'm Bobby, remember?"

"Yes, Bobby, I'll remember"

He stood up and said, "Come on, Kelsey. I want you to meet Jimmy, I'll show you where you can always find him. In fact, the two of you will be here more than me and the other guys."

Kelsey was led past the dispatcher desk, to a thick steel door which opened into the garage. She followed Bobby in and he pointed at a guy who straddled the motor of a big rig; his impact wrench in his hand. It seemed as though the shrill of his tool was ear piercing.

She almost winced at the sound when Bobby shouted, "Hey, Jimmy, before you get into whatever you're doing, I'd like you to meet our new dispatcher."

He stood up from his work and she thought, Oh my God. He was the handsomest man she'd ever seen. And almost immediately her heart started pounding in her chest. Her mouth went dry and lord help her, she couldn't seem to catch her breath.

Heavens, she couldn't let this guy, one of her bosses see her like this. She was acting as though she were a blithering idiot. So when the mechanic started down off the truck, she shouted, "No need."

She just climbed up the tire and reached her hand out to his. Their eyes met and for a moment they stood gazing at each other. She couldn't stop because his eyes seemed to sparkle with sensitivity and kindness, and decided she could sstare into them all day long. A moment later, he clasped her hand.

Looking way up, she decided he had to be six foot four, possibly more. His shoulders were wide and his waist was small. She swallowed hard when she saw his hair; it looked as though he'd just slid his fingers through it. She thought the look was great on him.

Reluctantly, she felt Jimmy slide his hand from hers and he stared down at it. She noticed then that her hand was greasy.

"Sorry about that," Jimmy said as he handed her a clean work rag.

"No big deal, it's only a little dirt." Kelsey wiped her hands as she beamed up at him.

"Maybe so, but most women wouldn't appreciate it," Jimmy confessed.

"This is Kelsey Curtis, our new dispatcher. I'm starting her today with a little info on how we work here at Big 4," Bobby said as he cleared his throat.

"It's nice to meet you, Jimmy," she said as she climbed down off the truck.

"The pleasure is all mine." He flashed her what she thought was a sexy smile.

"Okay, Kelsey, let's go back inside, I have a lot to teach you." Bobby led the way.

She followed him back towards the door, but before they reached it she wanted one last glimpse at Jimmy. So she turned around and their eyes met again. Kelsey smiled, he was checking her out, but she didn't dare continue to stare.

Heavens, he was one of her bosses. Get a grip, Kelsey. Then she tried to act as though it were nothing. By turning quickly and following Bobby back into the office.

A few moments later, Kelsey found herself at the dispatcher's desk. She was a little nervous; it had been a while since she'd been on the radio. But, her boss, Bobby, wanted her to get a feel for the way they did things. So Kelsey was getting a little practice by calling Benet.

"Benet, break for your new dispatcher. This is Kelsey, come back," she said with a little coaching.

Kelsey and Bobby only heard a deep, warm chuckle from the radio.

"Well, damn, I never thought Bobby was going to ever find us a dispatcher. Especially one with a sexy little voice. I can't wait to meet you, honey," Benet said.

"I'm no one's honey, Benet. My name is Kelsey and I'll work hard for you, but I won't be your honey."

Again, they heard his laughter fill the airwaves. "I understand, and I respect it, so Kelsey it is!" Benet agreed.

"I'll be starting a full day tomorrow, Benet, so we'll talk more then," she told him.

"That's a big 10-4. Have a good day little Miss Kelsey, and welcome to Big 4 Trucking," Benet declared.

Kelsey pulled off her headset, and she and Bobby couldn't help but laugh at Benet's response. Yet a moment later her laughter stilled in her throat. She had caught a glimpse of Jimmy, leaning against the open garage door, a huge smile on his face. Again she found herself trying to control her staring.

"Did we disturb your work, Jimmy?" Kelsey asked.

"No, I was just taking a little break."

Nervously, she nodded and went back to the paperwork Bobby had just explained to her.

A moment later, she saw him go to the door and stand next to Jimmy. She was being bad because she was trying to hear what they were saying, although she was only catching bits and pieces. Yet, it didn't stop her from straining to hear what they were saying.

"What do you think of her?" Bobby asked in a low voice.

"She sure isn't afraid to get her hands dirty," Jimmy observed.

"Yeah, she's taken to this job like a duck to water," Bobby said happily.

"What's her story?" Jimmy motioned his head toward Kelsey.

"She's fine with the money, and the hours, so we'll let it go at that. If she wants to tell us about herself, she will." Bobby shrugged.

Again Kelsey tried to act as though she didn't notice Jimmy staring at her. Truth was, she couldn't help but be nervous when someone as good looking as Jimmy paid her attention.

Her hands were shaking just a little when she overheard Bobby say, "Yeah, I'll stay in the office for the rest of the week to help her get adjusted, and off I go. So try to be good to this girl. I think she'll work out good for us."

"I agree, if anyone can do this job, its Kelsey." Jimmy motioned his head towards her again.

"I think you're right, Jimmy, yep, I think you're right," Bobby said.

Kelsey tried to hide the blush on her face by putting her head down. Still, she was surprised by their confidence in her. And as long as Jimmy didn't stare at her; she just might be able to do this job to their liking.

The next few days went well at Big 4 Trucking. It was near the end of the week when Trent came in to pick up the paperwork for a three day run, where he observed Bobby leaning over a young girl with spiked hair. Trent knew they'd hired a girl, and Bobby thought they would all get along—this had to be her.

Trent had spent the last few days organizing his and Candy's household. Although he knew the moment he left on his run she would try to do everything. He took a deep breath at the thought.

The truth was he'd have to settle for her just taking care of herself while he was home. He even gave his wife's two younger sisters orders to handle the housework. At their family meeting the whole family was excited about the new baby. Candy's sisters, Emma and Tess, vowed to do all they could for her, and their new little niece or nephew.

Trent smiled, because he found himself looking forward to being a dad. He would even try to be great at it. Their baby would be loved and cared for, if he had to shovel cow manure to make it happen. He even found himself wondering what their child would look like. Trent hoped the baby would have his wife's eyes and God help him, he also wanted his little one to have her beautiful smile.

Suddenly, Trent was drug back to Big 4, and the new dispatcher by Bobby's chuckle.

"Oh Trent, Kelsey Curtis, this is the last of the Big 4 partners. This is Trent Kelly, he and Benet are the big money making haulers."

Trent looked her up and down, and smiled. He knew by the look of her, she was tough, even though he knew he shouldn't judge her by her apperance. Yeah, she was going to fit right in.

He watched Kelsey walk straight across the room, and she stood right in front of him.

"I'm glad to meet you. I've heard lots about you. By the way, how's your wife? I hear she's expecting?" she said as she held her hand out to him.

Trent shook his head at Bobby as he grabbed hold of her hand and gave it a shake.

"And what exactly did Bobby tell you about me?" he said with suspicion.

"Just that you and Benet started this company, then you met Bobby in a bar. If I remember the story correctly, he talked you out of beating the hell out of him. You thought he was so good at it, you talked him into being not only a trucker for Big 4, but their salesmen as well."

Trent sat on the edge of Bobby's desk as he said, "I bet he didn't tell you he's one hell of a good driver himself, met him at a truck stop. He wouldn't shut the hell up about how he could sell anybody, anything. I wanted to kill him. But damn if he wasn't right, because he sold himself to Benet and me that night. Not only did we make him a partner, he'd also become a great friend."

"So you were all four friends?" Kelsey asked.

"Yeah, although Jimmy was another matter," Trent said.

"How did Jimmy get involved?" she asked.

"Trent here punched his last boss in the mouth," Bobby admitted with laughter in his voice.

"Now damn it, Bobby, you know the guy was lucky I didn't kill him," Trent confessed.

"Me, Benet and Trent went on a job—it was a long one, and all three of us shared the driving. The guys wanted me to sell us—Big 4, to a guy in Kentucky on our way. Anyway, we weren't more than twenty miles out of Kentucky when we had trouble with the truck. So we stopped at a little piss hole of a garage. Guess who worked there? None other than Jimmy," Bobby told her.

Trent began to chuckle as he took up the telling. "Man, he was wet behind the ears. Didn't know how to talk to people, and took all kinds of crap from the old man he worked for."

"We walked into the place in a big hurry. We had to be in Florida in two days and there was no time for delays," Bobby explained.

Trent took over the story. "Yeah, and there we sat with a truck that wouldn't move. So while I tried to calm Benet down, Bobby here started talking. I swear to you, that day alone, Bobby earned his share in Big 4."

"I tried to at least get the old man to look at the engine." Bobby told his side of the story. "I knew if I could find out what was really wrong with it the three of us could fix it, if we had to. Instead, I found out the old man didn't work on big rigs and he pointed to Jimmy. I swear to you, all I could see was the whites of his eyes." Trent and Bobby both started laughing.

"Yeah, and he was no more than twenty one," Trent said.

"No, Trent, he wasn't yet, remember, we took him drinking on his twenty first birthday, two months later."

"So what happened next?" Kelsey asked.

"The old man told Jimmy to get out there and look at the rig. He also told him not to fix it."

"Why don't they want it fixed?" Jimmy asked the man. That's when the old man hauled off and slapped the kid across the face and shouted, "Just do as you're told!" Bobby said as he shook his head.

Trent jumped right into the conversation. "I blew my stack. The kid didn't deserve to be hit, so without thinking I threw the old guy against the wall and yelled at him. 'If you hate us, fine, but you don't treat an employee like that!' I'm telling you, this guy showed no fear when he told us, 'he'll do what he's told, or he'll be out of a job.' I had to take my hands off the guy before I killed him."

"Well, once Jimmy came out with his tool box he slid under the truck. He was under there no more than twenty minutes when he came back out, smiling." Bobby went on. "It was just a bad hose. You were losing too much pressure. That's why it stalled out, I did a little patch job, should get you to the next town, just replace it and you'll be fine," Jimmy told us."

Trent continued the story. "Right there and then I knew he was the mechanic we needed. Our trucks were always breaking down, and the three of us could only do miner stuff, and none of us could diagnose a problem. So I said, "The old guy is an ass, come work for us."

Trent took a deep breath as he remembered out loud the conversation.

"One boss is as good as another, no, this is sure money. I'll be staying," Jimmy said.

"In that instant, I heard Bobby's voice ask, 'How about it guys?'"

"Of course we all thought it was a good idea, and seeing we agreed with a nod, it was unanimous. So, I asked, "How would you like to be a partner in our trucking company?" Trent chuckled.

"Like part owner?" the kid asked with eyes opened wide."

Trent explained it to him. "Yeah, you'll be our mechanic. If we make money, you make money. No one will slap you in the face again. We'll do things your way. Our garage will be run by you. You'll be king of your own domain."

"And I said, where do I sign? Got into their truck with only the clothes on my back, and my box of tools, and never looked back."

They all turned and saw Jimmy. He was standing in the doorway leading to the garage.

"You left your family and everything?" Kelsey asked.

"No, you see I was an orphan since I was little, making my way as I always did. Since then, Big 4 became my family. They were the only ones who ever cared about me. They've been my family, my brothers, and partners, all of 'em. If it wasn't for these guys I'd still be in that little good for nothing town, killin' myself and getting nothin for it. Here's where I belong," Jimmy said with pride.

"Well, you sure don't look like the filthy hick the guys made you out to be," Kelsey said.

"The guys, all three of them, taught me how to dress, take care of myself, but mostly they taught me how to be a man, and that's something I can never repay them for," Jimmy said with conviction.

"How long have you four been together?" Kelsey wanted to know.

"We chose the name Big 4 the day we came back with Jimmy. It was a unanimous decision," Bobby said.

"It will be four years come September," Jimmy said before anyone else could.

"Yeah, and none of us have looked back since," Trent announced.

3

Five p.m. came along at the end of a pretty quiet day. Kelsey was happy that tonight she would be home before eight. Finally, there would be time to go to the grocery store. She was thinking about what she was going to do with her first paycheck.

The long blue company check was being held tightly between her fingers. Then she thought about how this was going to help her start a new life; a life that didn't include the monster. She had her own apartment, a job, and money. She could now look forward to a life of her own. The thought put a big, satisfying smile on her face.

Until the front door opened, and a woman in her late thirties strutted in. She was wearing the tightest fitted skirt and blouse Kelsey had ever seen. The stretchy short black lace skirt left nothing to the imagination. The makeup on her face could only be described as being put on with a cement trowel. Her dark brown hair barely touched her shoulders, and it was as straight as an arrow. This was a look Kelsey could do without. However, she kept her thoughts to herself and asked in a calm tone, "Can I help you?"

"Who the hell are you?" the woman spat out.

"Excuse me?" Kelsey was taken aback.

"Where is Jimmy?" the woman said with an attitude.

"He's in the garage. I'll go tell him you're here. May I ask your name?" Kelsey said very business like.

There was a deep voice coming from behind them, and both women turned and saw Jimmy standing in the doorway.

"This is Tina Kutter," Jimmy said.

"I'm his girlfriend," Tina announced with a glare in Kelsey's direction.

In that instant Kelsey watched Tina slide in close to Jimmy and wrap her body around his. It was obvious she was showing Kelsey, Jimmy was *hers*. Although she could tell by the expression on his face, Jimmy was embarrassed by his girlfriend's sexual behavior in front of her.

It seemed to Kelsey, he was uncomfortable with the way she was behaving.

"This is our new dispatcher, Kelsey Curtis, and she's damn good at it," he said with a bit of apprehension.

Kelsey blushed at his praise.

"And all of us guys get along great with her. She also takes good care of Big 4 trucking. She's turning out to be just perfect for all four of us guys," he told Tina.

Kelsey gave Jimmy the cutest little smile; she was proud of what he thought of her abilities. She worked hard at being the perfect dispatcher. It was nice to know she was succeeding at it. Yes, she could almost feel her chest puffing up with the compliment.

So she said, "Thank you for noticing, Jimmy, I've been trying to do a good job."

She couldn't help but notice he gave her a half smile. She didn't realize her smile caught Tina's attention too.

"We have reservations, Jimmy. You promised to spend the whole night with me, remember?" She purred like a cat, or was it a cougar?

Kelsey observed that he never took his eyes off her when he said, "Go on, get out of here. You've been putting in lots of hours so I'll lock up."

She folded her pay check and placed it in her jeans pocket. "Thanks, Jimmy, I'll see you on Monday."

"Yeah, see you then."

Kelsey was on the other side of the full glass door looking for her car keys when she saw Jimmy walk away from Tina, went to the sink and washed his hands. She could tell by the look on Tina's face, she wasn't happy. Jimmy wasn't paying her any attention.

Kelsey's hand stilled in her purse as she heard Tina's voice through the door. Her voice dripped with seductive sweetness. It almost gave the little dispatcher a sugar rush, it was so sweet.

"I can see you like this new dispatcher person."

Kelsey watched Jimmy shrug. He had his back to her, but his voice came through the door just the same.

"She does everything we need done around here, and more. She handles the phone, and the guys on the road, which frees me up to fix trucks without interruption. Yeah, Kelsey does her job well, and she's not afraid to get her hands dirty. We need someone like her around here, Tina, a worker."

"I saw the way you looked at her. I can't believe you like that semi Goth look of hers," Tina snapped.

Standing outside, Kelsey could see Jimmy clearly. He seemed to know exactly how to handle this woman, because next he said, "Tina, she's a good employee, she treats all us guys good, speaks to us with respect. I think Kelsey should at least get that back."

Suddenly, he turned around and Kelsey saw his face and hands were washed. He walked right up to Tina and roughly pulled her into his arms where his lips covered hers, and he squeezed her bottom in both his hands.

Kelsey saw the look on Tina's face. If she didn't know better she would have sworn she was purring like a kitten, ready to play. Yes, it looked to her like Jimmy knew just how to handle this woman. But, truth be told, when he took hold of his girlfriend and squeezed her, Kelsey got hot all over. What was that all about?

She tried to shake off the feeling. Hell, this was spying on them. Truth was she didn't want to see anymore. But it was like watching a train wreck; you knew it would be terrible, and you should look away, but you just can't take your eyes off it.

So she watched him pull away from Tina, still holding her backside.

"Enough talk about Kelsey. Lets go to your house and you can help me shower, then we'll go out to dinner." He grinned devilishly at her.

Kelsey fumbled with her purse. Lord, they'd catch her out there watching them. Finally, she found her keys and ran for her car. She struggled to get the key in the door and fumbled with the ignition. Once it started she drove around the building. Hoping and praying she wasn't seen.

From the around the corner of the building she watched them pull away in Jimmy's truck. She took a big sigh of relief. It would have been terrible if they caught her watching them. To be honest, she didn't want to watch any more of Jimmy and Tina. It bothered her and she didn't even know why.

There was nothing between them. Or was there? The sight of his deep brown eyes did things to her. She could get lost in those eyes of his, and his dimpled smile could melt a snowman in minutes. Oh yeah, there was something smoldering just beneath the surface when it came to Jimmy. Or was she the only one feeling the heat?

Kelsey took a deep breath, as she tried to remind herself he wasn't her man. She was their dispatcher, nothing more. "Get a grip, girl."

Then she remembered the way he held Tina in his arms, put his hands on her bottom and pulled her close. A moment later she knew she was jealous. Because, oh how she wished she was in his arms just like Tina.

Monday morning came and Kelsey was at her desk going through the invoices when Trent, Benet, and Bobby came in the front door laughing and talking. They ended up sitting around Kelsey's desk. Getting their messages and mail, while they said hi to her.

"What did you do with your first pay check, Kelsey?" Trent was the first to ask.

"Bet she got drunker than a skunk, and spent it all at the bar." Bobby chuckled.

"No way, Kelsey's a smart girl. She paid bills, gassed up her car, maybe even stocked the house with some groceries," Benet said as a matter of fact.

"How did you know?" She stared at Benet.

"Benet's a good judge of people, always has been, and it looks like you're no exception to his judgment," Trent said.

"Is Jimmy here?" Bobby side-stepped the conversation for a moment.

"No. I haven't seen him since he told me to go home on Friday and he'd lock up. A girl named Tina came and picked him up."

"The Hoochi Mamma, huh?" Benet blurted out.

"Hoochi Mamma?" Kelsey echoed.

"Yeah, our good judge of character here gave her the name. Can you tell he doesn't like her?" Trent chuckled.

"Why do you call her that, Benet?" Kelsey asked.

"Because to put it delicately, she's a woman of very little morals, and she has an insatiable appetite for money. Jimmy's a good guy, and she knows she can get what she wants from him. And once she has every penny he's got, she'll leave him high and dry. I know this because I had my very own insight into a woman just like this, years ago. I learned the hard way. I sure would like to save Jimmy the heartache."

"Of what I saw of her, she seemed to be pretty possessive of Jimmy," she told them.

"I'm sure she doesn't want any other woman cutting in on her claim," Benet said with the shake of his head.

"Do you really believe that?" Kelsey questioned.

All the guys nodded. Just like Benet, the guys had their share of woman problems. They had a pretty good idea about this girlfriend of Jimmy's. Yet all they could do was stand back and hope he'd see it too.

"You met her. Was she nice to you?" Benet asked as he looked her in the eye.

All Kelsey did was look down.

"Just as I thought, she was a bitch to you, right?" Benet replied.

Kelsey didn't agree or disagree. It was true Tina was not a nice person, at least when she met her. However, she also thought it wasn't right to judge Jimmy's choice in women, so she said nothing.

Until she heard, "Kelsey's too nice of a girl to talk against anyone. We're putting her in a bad position. We won't bug you with this anymore," Bobby informed everyone.

The conversation was getting way too serious. Kelsey saw Trent pull a fifty dollar bill from the pocket of his jeans and hand it to her.

"Would you do me a favor and go get us all a coffee, even one for Jimmy? He'll need it when he comes in," Trent asked.

She slid the money in her pocket and headed for the door when Trent spoke again. "Don't forget yourself, and some donuts would really hit the spot."

With a big smile Kelsey opened the door and said, "You got it!"

Once she was gone, Trent turned on both his partners. "Look guys, this thing with Jimmy is getting out of hand. We have to back off the subject."

"What subject?" Trent turned at the voice; it was Jimmy. His eyes were barely open, and he looked like hell.

"You're the damn subject. Look at you. You look like you've been rode hard, and put away wet," Benet answered his question.

"Now what the hell is that supposed to mean?" Jimmy stepped right in and shouted.

Both men were eye to eye when Trent saw Bobby step between them.

"Look guys, we all have lots of work to do, let's forget about this crap."

The stance between both men suggested they were ready to come to blows. Which was obvious to Trent and Bobby.

Trent couldn't believe Jimmy just pushed Bobby out of the way and yelled, "I'm sick of this shit. You got something to say to me, Benet, just spit it out!"

"Alright, Jimmy, but remember you asked for it. You're always late, you pretty much look like hell all the time. You barely even care about the business here. All you care about is the Hoochi Mamma! You don't even see she's using you, man!"

Trent stepped into the middle of it when Jimmy grabbed a hold of Benet's shirt.

Now, Benet was the biggest of the guys. Then there was Trent, Bobby and Jimmy. All big guys mind you, but Trent knew if Jimmy kept pushing Benet, he would be the one in the hospital tonight. He shouted, "Enough!"

"Trent, he has no right to talk about my girlfriend like that," Jimmy roared.

"Jimmy's right, Benet. Who he sees is not our business," Trent reminded him.

A moment later Trent heard Benet growl out loud and Jimmy was smiling proudly, until Trent spoke. "You're right. Your girlfriend is none of our affair, but your work here is."

He leaned close to Jimmy. "Personally, I don't care if you bang the girl all night. Even if you two do it hanging from a chandelier, but being on time, and doing your job, is all of our business."

"But Trent…!" Jimmy tried to explain.

Trent held his hand up to Jimmy and went on. "What if I didn't come in and make my runs? What if Benet decided not to pick up his load on time? What if Bobby didn't show up on time for his meetings with our clients?"

"If I didn't drive we'd lose money. If Benet didn't get his load on time we'd lose the bonus, and if Bobby was late, our clients would figure we can't keep our promises. The same applies to you. You're responsibility is big. If these trucks don't run, we can't do all the things I just spoke of. We count on you to keep us on the road. You are the center of Big 4. Each one of us is important, that means you too. Every truck and every job hinges on you keeping us on the road. So, although you have a right to your own personal life, you also have a responsibility right here to Big 4." Trent took a deep breath.

At that point, Trent saw Kelsey come in the door, a smile from ear to ear.

"Coffee and donuts!" she announced.

The guys were staring at Jimmy, and the room was deafeningly silent.

"Not now, maybe later," Jimmy said, and into the garage he went with the slam of the door.

"Is everything okay?" Kelsey cringed.

"I don't know, is it guys?" Bobby glared at his partners.

Trent stared up at Benet. "Is it, buddy?"

"You got a coffee for me?" Benet said with a grunt.

Trent watched her hand him one, and to his office he went.

"What did I miss?" Kelsey said as she handed Bobby and Trent each a coffee.

"Trent and Jimmy had a little talk," Bobby answered her.

Without a word Trent took Jimmy's black coffee and went into the garage where Jimmy was stepping into his coveralls.

"You sure put me in my place. You happy?" Jimmy snapped.

"Look, kid, you know I think of all you guys as my brothers, you being my kid brother. I know how hard it is to juggle a relationship and Big 4 too."

"Yeah, but we all like Candy, she's the perfect girl for you. If you hadn't set your cap for her, I'm sure we would still all be fighting over her. So, you don't know what it's like to have the guys hate your girl."

"Hate's a pretty strong word, Jimmy." Trent shrugged.

"Then you use the appropriate word, and if you say Hoochi Mamma, so help me..." Jimmy said with frustration.

Trent chuckled. "It doesn't really have anything to do with what she's called. You see all three of us have been around the block, if you know what I mean. We've seen different types of girls, we've been through this. We just want to save you the heartache, really, that's all."

"You really think Benet cares about me?" Jimmy growled.

"He would have already broken your neck if he didn't. And if you haven't noticed, he's been cutting you months of slack over this."

"Trent…" Jimmy tried to explain.

All Trent did was hold his hand up for silence as he said, "Look, Jimmy, I'm not going to get into your life. If you want to talk, if you want someone to listen, you know where I am."

Trent handed Jimmy his coffee, and he nodded his head and Trent headed back into the office.

In that instant, Jimmy already had a pretty good idea he'd bitten off more than he could chew with Tina. He also knew if he talked to any of his partners it would be Trent. Still he wasn't ready to bare his soul to his friend, at least not just yet.

Jimmy leaned against the tool bench drinking his coffee as he gave his thoughts full rein over him.

He was thinking of Tina, and the weekend they'd just spent together. He'd been with her Friday and Saturday night, watching her drink herself out of her mind at the bar, the whole time insisting he join her in the drunken craziness. Then at three in the morning, when he couldn't participate any longer, the game was sex, hard and rough. He never imagined he'd find himself dreading sex, but as God as his witness he did with Tina.

What started out as a good time with no strings attached, turned into drudgery. Sex was no longer the pleasuring high it was at first. Damn, now he just wanted out. How in the hell was he going to pull that off? Tina wouldn't let this go, let it end. All she ever talked about was the two of them and how much she loved him. Damn, he was in one hell of a mess!

4

Kelsey saw Trent lead a lovely woman into the office of Big 4.

"Here she is, Candy. This is, Kelsey, our new dispatcher. Hell, she's more than that. She can do just about everything here. We've come to count on her for all sorts of things. Kelsey, this is my wife, Candy," Trent announced.

Kelsey held her hand out to his wife, and she took it.

"I'm so happy to meet you. The guys speak highly of you," Candy said as they shook hands.

Kelsey felt the heat of embarrassment flood her face. She knew her cheeks had to be bright red. All she could do was grin at Candy as she said, "It's nice to talk to someone who really knows these guys." She hoped to get the inside story.

"We'll talk!" Candy gave her an all knowing smile.

"But not now, my wife is going on a two day run with me." Trent grinned devilishly.

"Yeah, I literally had to take him to the doctor's office, so he could personally tell my husband I could go and drive," Candy qualified.

"Damn right." Trent grabbed hold of Candy's arm and led her through the door, Candy waving at her on the way out.

Kelsey watched Trent help Candy into the cab of the truck when a voice caught her attention. "What's with the color change?"

She turned and saw Jimmy. "What do you mean?" She sounded confused.

"Your clothes, they're different?"

"Oh." She looked down at herself; she was wearing tan jeans, and a tight tan blouse. "I thought a change once in a while would be nice. As much as I like black, sometimes it gets old."

"I see, but it does look good on you," Jimmy admitted.

"Why thank you." She knew she was blushing since her face felt hot. "Have we heard any word from Benet? I'm worried about his air brakes."

She tapped the headset on her head in her left ear. "No, come to think of it, I haven't heard from him since yesterday afternoon. Would you like me to call him?"

"No, if he has a problem, he'll call."

A couple of hours later a call came from Trent; he was losing oil pressure so she hurried into the garage, her headset on her head. She climbed up onto the engine of the big rig Jimmy was hip deep in at the moment.

"Jimmy, it's Trent. He's losing oil pressure."

She leaned over the engine and handed him the headset. Once the headset was on his head, he asked, "Yeah, Trent, what's happening?"

"I don't know. The truck just started losing pressure. Thank God I made it to a truck stop here in the upper peninsula."

"It's either one of two things, you either blew an oil pump, or you took a stone to the oil pan. So get under the truck, and tell me what you see under there."

"He says he doesn't see any holes in the oil pan, there isn't any oil dripping down there either." Candy spoke to Jimmy while Trent was under the truck.

"Alright, Candy, it has to be the oil pump. Where are you at?"

"Trent, where are we?" she asked.

"We're at the truck stop just outside of Iron Mountain." Trent took over the cell phone.

"How's it running? You think you can get her ten more miles?"

"I think I can if I take it easy, why?" Trent asked.

"Cause ten miles west of the truck stop, is Bad Dave's garage. The guy owes me," Jimmy explained.

"I remember Bad."

"Go there, tell him I sent you, and tell him to replace your oil pump."

"Have I told you lately what a pal you are?" Trent joked.

"Not lately, but I take what I can get. Now, get over to Bad. Call me and let me know how she's running." Jimmy chuckled.

"You got it, Jimmy!" Trent signed off.

Kelsey was admiring the smile on Jimmy's face when he handed her the headset. However, she was paying more attention to his wide grin than her footing. So when she leaned back to put the headset on, she lost her balance, and started falling backwards. Quickly Jimmy leaned over and grabbed hold of her so she wouldn't fall.

Although the only way he could do that was by grabbing hold of her bottom with both hands. A moment later she was being held close while she tried to steady herself.

Once she had a good footing again, she found herself staring into the most beautiful brown eyes she'd ever seen. All she could do was swallow hard.

"Thanks, Jimmy. I would have broken my fool neck." She took another swallow.

"You sure as hell would have. You have to be careful on these rigs," he warned.

A moment later she felt his hands—they were still holding her bottom. God help her but she was enjoying it. He smelled good too, even though he was full of grease, and why was her heart pounding? Heavens, her face had to be bright red because her cheeks felt like they were on fire. And what was this crazy feeling down deep inside her? She was frozen in place just staring at his beautiful eyes. It took her several moments to find the courage to stammer out, "You a… could… you know… let go of me now."

She saw something in his sweet expression; saw his sparkling eyes and up-turned lips. Made her think he just may have found her cute, maybe even funny. Could that be true? Still his hands were on her bottom, and she was embarrassed. Yet, the look on his face told her he was enjoying her bright red cheeks, and he wasn't letting go of her.

"I just want to make sure you don't fall." His grin turned devilish.

"Jimmy, I'm okay, so you can let go of me!" she insisted.

A deep chuckle seemed to fill the garage, and she felt him move his hands from her butt, take hold of her hand and ease her down off the big rig. When her feet hit the floor, he let go, and she smiled up at him.

"Thanks a…a…again, Jimmy," she stammered out.

"No sweat, Kelsey." He winked at her.

She walked away to the sound of his laughter. What was so funny? Heat permeated her body, top to toe as she imagined him staring at her backside. She couldn't help but smile at the thought. It made her feel just a little sexy. Perhaps Jimmy was a butt man, and a giggle got caught in her throat. Yes, she couldn't help but hope he liked the look of her from behind. Because each time she looked back, his eyes seemed to sparkle with devilment. Oh, how she wished she knew what he was thinking.

Once she reached the door, she took one last look back at Jimmy, just in time to see him take a deep breath and go back to his work. Kelsey was happy, because maybe, just maybe, he found something attractive about her.

It was nearly six pm as Kelsey stood filing the old invoices when a familiar voice broke the silence.

"Who the hell had their hands on your ass?" Tina shouted.

Kelsey turned and tried to see what she was talking about, but she couldn't. So she shrugged and said, "Oh, it must have been from Jimmy's hands, you see, I almost fell off a truck and Jimmy saved me."

"Are you talking about my Jimmy? You better keep your hands off my man, or you'll be sorry," Tina hissed.

"Hey, I don't have to explain anything to you," Kelsey informed her. Tina gave Kelsey a push, but she held her ground, and pushed her back, just in time for Jimmy to walk in.

He scowled. "What's going on?"

"Nothing, Jimmy. Your girlfriend is just a little crazy jealous."

Before Kelsey knew it, Tina turned her around as she tried to show him the hand prints on the back of the dispatcher's slacks.

"What the hell is this, Jimmy?" Tina demanded.

"Let go of Kelsey."

"I won't take this crap!" Tina yelled.

"You better shut up right now, Tina. Nobody here has done anything wrong; I won't be accused of anything. If you don't trust me, then…?" He left the rest hanging.

"No Jimmy, I didn't mean… I just wanted her to know, I won't have her coming on to you." Tina seemed nervous.

"Look Tina, nothing happened, so leave Kelsey alone. This discussion is over!"

"Alright, baby, I won't cause any more trouble," Tina said as she ran her fingers over his shoulder.

Kelsey stood quiet as she watched Jimmy give his girlfriend a serious glare, and immediately the woman changed the subject.

"I really came here to tell you I made reservations at our favorite restaurant," Tina said as sweet as sugar.

Kelsey noticed Jimmy look over at her, and she tried to act indifferent to the whole thing.

"I'll go change, and we'll go. If you're through with your accusations, that is?" he threatened.

"You know I trust you, baby, and if you say this is all innocent, I'm sure it is." She moved her fingers over his shoulder seductively.

"Good, I'll be right back."

Kelsey no sooner saw Jimmy go through the garage door when Tina pushed her against the file cabinet.

"Don't think I don't know you're trying to take my man. Let me tell you something, if you continue this, you'll be sorry."

Kelsey gave her a push and Tina staggered back. "Listen, girl, you know nothing about this company, and I don't need your permission for what I do. I talk to who I like, when I like, because I work here. It's my job to talk to Jimmy when needed. I'm not going to stop just because you say so. You're not the boss of me, Tina!"

A moment later she saw Jimmy walk in, and Tina looked as though she had just been waiting patiently there for him.

"Good night, Kelsey, see you tomorrow," he said as he took hold of Tina's hand.

Kelsey never changed her expression when Tina gave her a dirty look. All Kelsey said was, "See you tomorrow, Jimmy.

Kelsey smirked at Tina until they were out the door. She didn't realize she was messing up Tina's plans to have Jimmy all to herself.

She didn't have any idea the kind of trouble the girlfriend was cooking up for her. Yes, Kelsey should have been worried.

Jimmy was parked outside of Tina's apartment. He was waiting for her to fetch a jacket because she was cold. Even tried to get him to come inside with her. Hell, that would only lead to drinking and sex at her place. A steak is what he craved. He was starving. Seemed like sleep and food wasn't something his girlfriend ever needed. He leaned his head back against the headrest of his truck and closed his eyes. Right now a big juicy steak and a good night's sleep sounded wonderful. He laughed out loud. Damn, when was the last time he'd trade food and sleep for a sure thing? He just shook his head.

Before long, Jimmy found himself thinking about work and Kelsey. A big grin took over his face at the thought of his hand prints on her cute little butt. Man, she was soft, warm and awfully appealing.

Truth was he enjoyed the sight of his hand prints on her bottom. Yeah, he could hold on to her all day long. He shook his head again. No, he wouldn't act on his feelings, not with Kelsey, especially when he was still in a relationship with Tina. It just wouldn't be right to either one of them. Damn it, he had some decisions to make.

Suddenly, he was caught off guard when the truck door opened and he saw Tina step inside.

"What's with the long face?" Tina asked with a sweet smile.

"Nothing, I'm just starving. Aren't you hungry? I know you do computer work from home, and eat very little, but still, it's almost 6:30, and I haven't eaten since noon. I'd wager you haven't eaten all day."

"Yeah, I guess I could eat." She shrugged.

Jimmy put the truck in reverse and backed out of the parking space, and headed out onto the road without a word.

5

Two more weeks had passed and Kelsey was doing great at her new job. She was beginning to really like the guys she worked for. Especially Jimmy; there was just something about him. The way he smiled at her when she went in the garage to ask him something, or when she thought about how close he seamed to stand next to her. Heaven help her but she found herself struggling with her emotions.

Although her response to him was the only thing that puzzled her; the quickening of her heart beat, the sweaty palms. God help her, sometimes she couldn't even catch her breath. To say nothing about how her body reacted around him. It was as though she had no control over herself, and if he were to accidentally rub against her, heat surged through her, and she became breathless. Sometimes answering his simplest questions became a battle between her mind and her body.

She put her feelings aside; she was happy because today she got her first invitation to have some fun with her bosses, although it didn't start that way.

Bobby walked into the Big 4 office with Trent. He should have been dog tired from the two day haul but he wasn't, and he felt great—so great he was telling jokes.

Truth was his thoughts were all about Torrie; she was coming home for the weekend and he was excited to see her. Seemed he always was happy to see the cute little blonde. Even after a year of seeing her only now and then, he was still attracted to everything about her. And the thought of spending the whole weekend with her had his heart pounding a wild beat.

Bobby took a deep breath, because suddenly he was pulled from his thoughts by Kelsey.

"What's with Bobby? Does he have a hot date tonight, or something?" she asked.

"No, actually he's coming over to my house tonight. We're going to play some cards, have a few drinks, probably order some pizza. You're welcome to join us, Kelsey," Trent encouraged.

"I'd love to, thanks for the invite."

Bobby headed for the bathroom while they spoke. And it wasn't long before he came out looking like another man. He was clean shaven, wearing a clean crisp baby blue dress shirt which seemed to match his eyes. Perfectly fitted jeans with shiny black boots finished off his great look, and he smelled wonderful too.

"Does he always look this good and smell so nice for cards?" Kelsey asked.

"He does when Torrie comes to town." Trent chuckled.

"Who's Torrie?"

"My sister-in-law," Trent told her.

"That's not true, Trent, I always come over when you ask me," Bobby interrupted.

"Yeah you do, but you are only this happy when Torrie's in town," Trent qualified.

"So, Bobby has a thing for your sister-in-law?" Kelsey smiled.

"I don't have a thing for her, we're just friends," Bobby informed her.

"You and I both know you've got a thing for Torrie. If it weren't for her going to school, you know there would be something going on between the two of you." Trent couldn't help but put his two cents in.

"You know, now's not the time as well as I do. So just let things stay like they are," Bobby snapped.

"You're an ass for not telling her how you feel," Trent snapped back.

"Maybe so, but until she's done with school, we stay like this. And Trent, just keep your mouth shut!" Bobby demanded.

"You're in love, Bobby," Kelsey told him.

"I never said I was in love." Bobby grinned and placed his finger on her nose. "C'mon, Kelsey. You don't even know what that means."

"You might think that about me, but I know about this stuff." She acted knowledgeable.

"And just what do you think you know about love?" Jimmy's voice came across the room.

"I'm not a little girl, nor am I stupid about what men want. They want sex, plain and simple!" Kelsey informed him.

"I guess you do know what men want." Bobby lifted an eyebrow at her comment.

"So, you have experience with men?" Jimmy questioned.

"I didn't say that, Jimmy. I said I knew what men wanted. And asking about my experience is a pretty personal question, don't you think?" She nodded for emphasis.

"Hey, Kelsey, you're the one handing out information." Jimmy grinned.

Kelsey took a deep breath, because what she said next was rotten and she knew it the moment it came out of her mouth. But hell, she said it anyway.

"We all know little Tina is giving you exactly what you want. Because it couldn't be her brains you're seeing her for!" she said with a little jealousy in her tone.

The look in his eyes made her blood run cold. She knew he was angry, there was no mistaking his look.

Kelsey was totally prepared to take the licken she knew she was about to get for her stupid remark. Damn, why didn't she just keep her big mouth shut?

Now, Kelsey knew everything she said was true enough. However, she also realized Jimmy was dating Tina, and he would feel compelled to defend her honor.

Yeah, she figured Tina deserved every rotten word. So when she saw the look in his eyes she also knew he wouldn't let her make these type of remarks. With wide eyes she watched him approach her.

However, at that precise moment, Kelsey saw Trent step between them, and she took a deep sigh of relief.

"Now, Jimmy, you were getting a little personal," he said as he leaned close so only Jimmy could hear. "Hell, Jimmy, she's a great office worker, and the best dispatcher we've ever had. So, I'm begging you not to kill her," Trent said in a near whisper.

"I'm not going to kill her, I would never lay a finger on a girl, you know that. I just want to see how far she'll go with this." Jimmy grinned.

"Okay, but remember we still have to work with her." Trent gave him a smile and a wink.

Kelsey saw Trent step out of the way, and when Jimmy's eyes met hers she immediately looked at the floor.

She was totally aware of the fact Jimmy wasn't going to give into the silent regret when he took two steps toward her and lifted her chin so she'd look up at him.

"You have no right to talk about my girlfriend. I know sometimes she comes off a little rough around the edges," Jimmy said.

Kelsey wanted so much to say, that's an understatement. But his hand was already under her chin. She just listened to him go on.

"However, it still remains I am seeing this girl, which makes her my personal business, got it?"

She didn't answer him immediately so he repeated, "Got it?"

"Yes, Jimmy," she finally said.

He was about to let go of her when she just couldn't let it lay. "So, you're going to give me the same consideration?"

Kelsey watched the confusion appear on his face. Which made her just a bit braver.

"You don't talk about my boyfriend either," she said to get under his skin.

"I don't understand. I didn't think you had a boyfriend?" Jimmy asked.

Kelsey saw something in his eyes, She thought he seemed to be searching her eyes for an answer only she could give. For a moment, he even looked a little worried. Was it wrong of her to want him to be as jealous as he looked?

However, all she did was stir the pot a little more and see where it took her.

"Pretty presumptuous of you, wasn't it? Just because I don't bring him around, doesn't mean I don't have one."

"She's got you there, Jimmy."

"Shut up, Bobby! So, you have a boyfriend? When and where did you meet him? Do I know the guy? Have you been with him long?" Jimmy's eyes even questioned her.

"I didn't say I had a boyfriend." She side stepped that one.

"Then what the hell are we talking about?" Jimmy raised his voice.

"Respect. You want it, and I think I should have it too!" She didn't know why, but she was enjoying her banter with Jimmy.

She watched him shake his head, and give her slow grin. It seemed as though he was glad she didn't have anyone in her life. A moment later the conversation was ended, because Kelsey saw Trent slap Jimmy on the shoulder.

"You're not getting anywhere, let's go play cards," Trent told him.

At that point she saw Bobby put his arm around Jimmy's shoulder and he was led out the door.

"I'm still expecting you to come play poker with us," Trent said as his hand was on the door handle.

"I think I kind of got under Jimmy skin, so maybe now's not a good time." She shrugged.

"Look, Kelsey, Jimmy knows you were messing with him. He'll be fine by the time we get to my house."

She nodded as Trent headed for her desk. He jotted down his address and phone number, folded the paper and handed it to her. "Here's my address and if you have any trouble finding it, call."

"But..."

"No buts, be there, lock up and come over. I'm expecting you."

"Alright, I'll be there," she agreed.

Kelsey took a deep breath. She liked Jimmy a lot, even more than she should. A grin filled her face, because getting him all riled up was kind of exciting. Although maybe she'd taken their loud conversation a bit too far.

The truth was she wanted to see his reaction to her having a boyfriend. She wasn't disappointed either. It really did seem to bother him. Yet she couldn't be quite sure how he felt about another man, but he sure did get agitated.

A giggle slipped out of her mouth as she thought about how jealous he seemed to be when she brought up the subject of her having a boyfriend. She shrugged; maybe he liked her just a little. She sure hoped he did because the rapid beat of her heart was still pounding in her ears from their heated discussion.

Even when he seemed to be angry, she knew he would never hurt her. There was no way she could know that, but she did. People's eyes were the windows to the soul, and through his eyes she only saw kindness.

Kelsey took a deep breath. How she wished she could have a chance with Jimmy. But Hell, he was her boss, and he also had a girlfriend—a pretty jealous one. "Oh Jimmy, why do you have to be seeing Tina?"

Suddenly she was pulled away from her thoughts when the switchboard lit up and a deep voice filled the room.

"Kelsey, this is Benet, I have a problem."

"I'm sorry, Benet, but all the guys went to Trent's house to play cards. If you give me twenty minutes, I'm sure I can get a hold of them," she assured him.

"No Kelsey, it's you I need. I'm an hour away and by mistake I took a sinus pill for night time, and I'm having a hell of a time staying awake," Benet explained.

"Alright, Benet, lets talk," she spoke calmly.

"Talk about what?" He yawned.

"Tell me all about yourself. Tell me how you and Trent met?"

A chuckle came from the other end of the radio when Benet said, "Hell, he was only twenty, and I wasn't much older. We both had trucks we were trying to pay off. It also seemed we had runs coming and going in the same towns. We were always running into each other. We even liked the same diners and bars. Before we knew it, we were talking. Trent's father was a no account, all the man cared about was the bottle. He sure did like his liquor, even more than his kids, took to beating him too. Trent could have gone either way, could have turned out like his old man, or the good guy he has become. Thank God the experiences in his life made him a good person," he told her.

"What about you, was your home life good?" she wondered out loud.

"Hell no, not much better than Trent's, but in my case, it was my mother who was the no account. My dad was a hard working man who worked ten to twelve hours a day, just to keep a roof over our heads and food in our bellies. Mama… Well she was a drunk who would lay down with any man for her booze. I was fourteen when my mama brought the last man home to party with.

Thank God I wasn't home. My little brother and I were coming from school when my daddy got home and found her. I didn't know it at the time, but he'd already killed her, and the man she took up with.

When I got home from school, daddy was rocking on the front porch, his rifle over his lap. I swear to you, I'll never forget the look in his eyes. He told me to go to my Granny's and stay with her, he'd come for us later. I thought it was strange, yet my daddy would never take any sass, so I didn't give him any. That was the last time I saw him, he shot himself that afternoon. At least that's what the sheriff told my Granny." Benet went quiet.

"So, what happened to you and your brother?" She worried when he yawned again and she blurted out, "Benet?"

"I'm still here, Kelsey. Damn, you're a good listener, its been a long time since I told anyone this."

"Doesn't matter, Benet. You need to keep awake."

She listened as he took a deep breath and went on.

"My Granny finished raisin' us, and she was getting on in age. So when I got old enough to handle a truck I took to driving. I used to be pretty handy at fixing the old rigs, that's how I got my first. Bought an old rig, fixed it up, and off I went."

"How did you hook up with Trent?" She was curious.

"Seems Trent and I both got wind of a cross country job. The haul would run every three months, and the money was great. Well, we both showed up for the job. The guy was an older man and he left it to us to settle it. So Trent and I had a drink and talked it over. Once we got talking, I realized my old rig wouldn't take it. We had to go from California to New York in eight days, that meant nonstop driving because of the route. Trent's truck was newer, but he wasn't a good mechanic, and there was the time frame. For an eight day trip, two guys would have to rotate sleeping to get there on time."

"So you shared?"

"Yep, we used his truck, I did the maintenance, we shared the driving, and Big 4 began."

"Is that what you first named it?" she asked.

"Hell no, it was gonna be Big Rig Trucking, but Bobby came along, and we needed Jimmy, so Big 4 was born."

Candy was waiting at home when the guys from Big 4 came in the back door. Once her husband came in she wrapped her little pregnant body around Trent. She giggled when he lifted her off the floor and hugged and kissed her. Once she was back on her feet again, she gave Bobby and Jimmy a hug hello. Candy loved the guys and she knew they cared deeply for her and Trent too.

Although, when she hugged Bobby, she whispered, "Torrie's home, but she's got a date."

"Who the hell is she going out with?" He raised his voice.

"All I know is he's from around here." She shrugged.

At that moment the doorbell rang and Candy gave Bobby a sad look. "That has to be him now."

"I'll get the door for Torrie." He gave her a big smile.

Candy turned to Trent at the same time Bobby headed for the living room. "I thought he was going to be upset, not welcome the guy in!" she told her husband.

Candy saw Trent give Jimmy an all knowing smile, and they both started laughing. "What's so funny?"

"You'll see, baby, you'll see." Her husband grinned.

So she watched Bobby head for the front door, wearing tight jeans, a pressed blue dress shirt, and his leather jacket was open.

From the kitchen Candy observed Bobby as he opened the door for a guy who couldn't be more than twenty two.

"I'm here to see Torrie," the young man said.

Candy wanted to laugh at the way Bobby towered over the guy when he put his arm around his shoulder.

"Are you sure you want to see, Torrie? Didn't you know she's a married woman?" he said seriously.

"Why, no, she's never said anything about being married. Are you sure about this?" the young man asked.

"Yeah I'm sure, because she's my wife." Bobby patted the guy on the shoulder.

Candy could see by the look on Bobby's face, he wanted to laugh at how quickly the guy went white and backed away from him.

"Why would she agree to go out with me if she's married?" He seemed confused.

"You see, she's always trying to make me jealous," Bobby said as he leaned close to the guy. "She loves to get me mad, just so we can make up."

"I'm so sorry, Mr.... Mr...." he stuttered out.

"Weston, Bobby Weston."

"Well, Mr. Weston, I won't be bothering you anymore," and he all but ran out the door.

Bobby laughed when he spotted Trent leaning against the kitchen doorjamb.

"I knew you had something like this up your sleeve. Now what the hell are you going to tell Torrie?" Trent said.

A moment later Bobby turned at the sound of a voice he knew very well.

"Tell me what?"

He looked over and there Torrie stood. Bobby couldn't help but gaze at the beautiful blonde hair that hung over her shoulders. Hip hugger jeans had him staring because they hugged her hips tightly. Those jeans showed the small little round shape of hers off beautifully. A low cut, fitted knit long sleeved shirt covered those full round breasts that seemed to call out to him. God, Bobby wanted to touch her all over while he covered her painted red lips with his. However, all he did was take a ragged deep breath.

"Tell me what, Trent?" she repeated.

"You'll have to ask Bobby. He talked to the guy." Trent shrugged

So he folded his arms across his chest as he and Torrie waited to hear what Bobby had to say.

"Well, Torrie, it's quite simple, your date. The guy simply just changed his mind." Bobby shrugged.

"And why would he change his mind?" Now she folded her arms across her chest and gave him a serious glare.

"Yeah, Bobby, why would he do that?" Trent asked with a wide grin.

"Trent, I'm talking to Torrie, butt out!" He raised his voice.

Bobby saw Trent shrug his shoulders and head back into the kitchen.

"He just changed his mind. A person has the right to do that, don't they?" Bobby tried to explain.

"I just spoke to him an hour ago. What did you say to him, Bobby?" Torrie demanded.

"You know, Torrie, I'm disappointed in you. You're accusing me of doing something underhanded. I thought we were friends?"

"Bobby..." She tried to get a word in.

He just held his hand up to her. "You hurt my feelings."

"I didn't mean to hurt your feelings, but this all seems pretty strange," she said, confused.

A moment later he was holding her in his arms as he asked, "Where's my hello Bobby kiss? I thought we were buds, I've missed my good buddy." He grinned when she went up on tip toes and gave him a friendly little kiss, however, that was all the encouragement Bobby needed. He couldn't help but take her sweet little kiss to where passion lived. When he was done with her, he litterly had to hold her up.

"That guy is no loss, Torrie. You need a man, not a punk. You need someone who will set you on fire," he whispered softly in her ear.

"So, you did have something to do with him leaving?" Her eyes opened wide.

"All I said was you needed a man. Now, let's go play some cards. I can't wait to hear what you've been up to at school. Oh, and if you'd wear shoes instead of those damn flip flops, you wouldn't have to stretch so far to kiss me."

"Bobby!" She smacked his shoulder.

"You know I'm right." He winked at her.

"One of these days, Bobby Weston…" she growled.

Before she could utter another word, he slid his open palm over her exquisite round derriere and said, "One of these days you're going to give me more than just a kiss, right Torrie?"

"One of these days I'm going to strangle you!" she snapped as she yanked his hand off her rear.

His only answer was a deep chuckle as he pulled her into the kitchen to play cards.

The whole table was deep into the poker game when Kelsey knocked at the back door. She smiled as a lovely woman with a beautiful smile opened the door.

"Is this Trent and Candy Kelly's house?" she asked.

"Yes, it is. I'm Candy's sister, Torrie. C'mon in."

Kelsey stepped in and the first person she saw was Jimmy, who gave her a wink.

"What took you so long?" Trent asked.

She focused on Trent, "I got a call from Benet. Seems he took a night time sinus pill and needed to talk to someone so he could get home without falling asleep."

"Is he alright?" Bobby asked with concern.

"Yeah, I talked to him until he pulled into the truck yard. I also drove him home, even made sure he got to his bedroom. Locked him in the house, and came right here."

"You see, Jimmy; I told you Kelsey's irreplaceable," Trent informed him.

"Yeah, she is definitely a keeper." Jimmy smiled over at her.

"Even after I got under your skin earlier?" she prodded.

"Yeah, we can have our misunderstandings, Kelsey, but it doesn't mean you're not a great dispatcher," he confessed.

"So, can we have a truce?"

"Yep, a truce it is, Kelsey!"

"Enough of the Kelsey fan club. Sit down, girl, it's your deal!" Trent interrupted.

Kelsey sat down when Bobby slid another chair across the kitchen. Everyone was still chuckling when she shuffled the deck of cards in her hands competently.

I think we have a pro here," Bobby said to Torrie.

And a moment later, Kelsey announced, "The name of the game is seven card Stud," and the game began.

6

Monday came quickly for Kelsey. All of Big 4 Trucking played cards until four in the morning on the Saturday before. So she spent the better part of the next day sleeping. Still, Sunday was full of laundry and errands, and after sleeping late into the day, she finally arose and did her chores. However, she didn't mind; she found not only did she like working for these guys, she enjoyed playing with them too. Plenty of laughs made a good time even better.

Suddenly her thoughts went to Jimmy, Kelsey couldn't keep her eyes off him all night at the poker game. She sighed.

She thought his style of card playing was unique. Especially the way he slung his arm over the back of his chair as he played. And oh my God when he smiled, she could feel her heart pounding in her chest, which made concentration difficult at best. Yet even under those conditions, she was able to take quite a bit of her boss's money. Enough to do all her grocery shopping on it, and enough money left to buy the new shoes she'd been drooling over for a month now.

She was silently thanking her brothers for teaching her poker, and showing her how to bluff.

With thoughts of her brothers came memories of the monster, her brother, Josh. He had turned into a mean man. Booze and drugs were his only friends. She'd spent the last six years trying to find a job in a place where he couldn't find her. Josh felt Kelsey was his meal ticket. She'd worked since she was fifteen, just to have it all taken away by Josh.

As Kelsey unlocked the door to Big 4 she remembered her last good job as a cab dispatcher in Detroit. It was a good job. She made a good living too. But once her check was cashed on Friday, her brother would be waiting for her at the apartment, so he could take it all. That's why she always paid her rent and bought food before she even came home, because she knew Josh would take it from her, rent and all.

Kelsey was making coffee when she thought about the last time she saw Josh. It was in Detroit, in the apartment. She decided she was done working, only to hand over every penny of her check to Josh. So on payday, when her brother came in to take her money, she refused to give it. He nearly beat her to death before she told him where the money was. She was out of work for nearly a month, and it took her nearly that long to stand again. Although once she could, she worked one more week. Only long long enough to afford a ticket for a bus out of town.

In the last six years, she worked any job she could find. Never stayed long enough anywhere to be found by Josh. It was the reason she didn't allow herself to put down roots. Because she knew once she did, Josh would find her, and take all she had away from her.

She knew if he found her again, he'd take everything she'd saved, then he'd beat the hell out of her. Now she was praying she'd gotten far enough away from him, so she'd never be found. Because for her to give up all she worked for, he would have to kill her.

Kelsey was pulled from her thoughts when the door opened and Bobby walked in, whistling, and she couldn't help but file Josh away and give Bobby a smile.

"Stop smiling, Kelsey."

"Why?"

"Because I hate a winner who gloats," He tried to act serious.

"I'm not gloating, although I was the big winner on Saturday." She giggled.

"You see, right there Kelsey, you're gloating." He wagged his finger at her.

"Alright, I'll change the subject. Why are you smiling and whistling, you were the biggest loser?" she prodded.

"Bobby doesn't care about the money…he cares about Torrie. And if I can judge the smile on his face, I'd wager he spent the weekend at Trent and

Candy's, drooling over Torrie," Jimmy joked as he leaned against the front door.

Kelsey turned to Jimmy as she watched him walk in and sit on the edge of Bobby's desk."

How do you know about this? Did you see him there?" she asked.

Her eyes followed Jimmy across the room.

"Exhibit A" and he pulled on the shirt under Bobby's leather jacket.

"This is how I know; he left here Friday night, wearing the very same shirt. So, it's logical he didn't go home."

"You wore the same shirt for three days?" Kelsey was appalled.

"I washed my shirt yesterday, wore Trent's clothes on Saturday," Bobby explained.

"I rest my case!" Jimmy said like an expensive lawyer.

"You really do like her, don't you?" She giggled.

"Yeah, for all the good it does me." Bobby shrugged.

"Have you told her how you feel?" She seemed concerned.

"Look, Kelsey, I'll tell you this once and we won't talk about it again. Torrie's going to be a doctor, It's always been her dream, I may be a shit, but I can't go after her now. She has to get what she's worked for so hard."

"I watched you two while we played cards. Neither one of you could keep your eyes off the other. It just seems like a crying shame to me." She shook her head.

"Drop it, Kelsey, this is not open for discussion," he said.

She patted him on the back. "Okay, Bobby, I'll drop it."

"You know, Kelsey, we have to have another poker game soon, because I have to get some of my money back," Jimmy said as he poured a cup of coffee.

"You're just pissed because you got beat by a girl!" Bobby chuckled.

"Her being a girl had nothing to do with it. I hate losing my money to anyone," Jimmy insisted.

"I'd be happy to play cards with you whenever you like," she agreed.

"You're on." Jimmy toasted her with his cup of coffee.

She stood there until Jimmy stepped into the garage. Once the door was closed behind him, she said, "He seems happy today, rested even."

"Looks like he didn't see Tina this weekend." Bobby's voice was soft.

"Why wouldn't he? They're an item, aren't they?" She raised an eyebrow.

"I've tried real hard to stay out of all the guys' lives. It's safer that way." Bobby shrugged.

Kelsey went to the dispatcher's desk as Bobby made his way to his desk and some contracts. She was wondering what changed Jimmy? Today, like the night they played poker, he seemed happy, pleasant, even, now he had her curiosity peaked.

Although, her curiosity didn't last long, because a few moments later, Tina came in with a slam of the door, and Kelsey and Bobby looked up at her. However, it was only Kelsey she questioned.

"Where the hell is Jimmy?" Tina said with an attitude.

All Kelsey did was point at the door that divided the office from the garage and watched as Tina stormed past her and hurried into the garage, slamming the door behind her.

A moment later, Kelsey could hear shouting. She stood right behind Bobby, who was listening to their conversation at the open crack of the door. Truth was she couldn't make out a word. She was hoping Bobby was getting it all. Until suddenly their voices went up, and it was crystal clear.

"Jimmy Ray, where the hell were you all weekend? You told me you were taking me out to dinner on Saturday. You know we always spend the weekend together," she shouted.

"No, Tina. You said we were. I never said I was going out with you on Saturday night." Jimmy's voice was firm.

"I thought you and I were building a strong relationship?" She sounded pitiful.

"Tina, I care about you, but damn it, girl, I need a little time for myself!" he said with irritation.

"So what did you do all weekend, other than ignore my phone calls?" Her hands were on her hips.

"You know Tina, you're really starting to piss me off, just go do your computer work at home, I'll call you later!"

"I quit my job. I thought you would move in with me, and I'd spend my time taking care of you."

"I'm sorry, Tina, but you better go back to your boss and beg for your job back. Because I'm not moving anywhere, nor are you going to take care of me!"

"But Jimmy…?"

"You're pushing me, Tina. Just get out of here," he warned.

"Couldn't I just work here? I'm sure I can do something. Maybe you could get rid of Kelsey, and I'll be your dispatcher." She sounded desperate.

"First off, you don't know a thing about dispatching, secondly, the hiring of help is Bobby's job, thirdly and frankly, I don't want you here."

"Why on earth don't you want me working here?"

"Because we'd just get on each other's nerves, and I don't want you keeping tabs on everything I do. Now, get out of here. I'll call you later." he barked.

"You promise, maybe we could go to dinner?" she pleaded.

"Damn it Tina, I'll call you!" he shouted.

Tina stared into his stern eyes. She didn't know what had come over him. It seemed as though she could always control Jimmy, a little sex, and he was hers. That was it; she had to get him back into her bed. She'd play the good little girlfriend, bide her time until he was back in her power again.

So she decided there would be no pushing him. Her plan to keep Jimmy happy, and with her, was the idea. Yes, Tina would do what she did best. Entice him with her love making. No man could resist her in bed.

Tina looked into his eyes and didn't say another word. Making him even more angry than he was wouldn't help her case right now. So, she just nodded to him and headed for the door.

Kelsey hurried away and Bobby followed her. Before they knew it, Tina had stomped into the office, Kelsey didn't pay any attention to the noise she was making. She just stood there staring at Jimmy's girlfriend.

"What are you looking at?" Tina asked with an attitude.

"I'm looking at a woman who's struggling to keep her man," Kelsey blurted out.

Kelsey knew she shouldn't have made the comment as soon as the words were out of her mouth. But heaven help her, Tina was never nice to her. Hell, the very first thing she said to her was "Who the hell are you?"

Kelsey'd been yelled at, pushed into file cabinets, and talked down to by this woman. So if she could make her mad, she would.

Yet a moment later, Kelsey truly regretted her comment. Because Tina brought out her worse fear.

"Everyone has something they fear, something that haunts them. I'm going to find out what yours is, and God help you, I'm going to rub your nose in it. You don't try to take what's mine, and not pay a huge price for it!" Tina said with venom in her voice.

"Listen, honey, I'm not chasing Jimmy, and if you remember it's you who started on me just because I work here. You even thought something was going on because he tried to save me from falling off a big rig. If you have a problem with that, it's your problem, not mine. So just get off my back and stay off!" Kelsey argued.

Without another word, Kelsey watched Tina storm out the door.

Once the woman was gone. Her thoughts turned to Josh. Could Tina find out about him? No, even if she did, there's no way she could find out about what he'd done to her, no, Tina was all talk.

The rest of the day went off without a hitch, until Kelsey got a call from Trent, who was an hour outside of town. He needed to talk to Jimmy.

Kelsey walked into the garage shouting for Jimmy, who shouted back at her from a creeper underneath the Peterbilt big rig he was now repairing. So she grabbed the other creeper leaning against the wall, and slid under the truck next to him. The sight of Kelsey rolling under the truck had Jimmy chuckling.

"What's up, Kel?" he asked.

"My name is Kelsey."

"I know Kel, what's up?" he teased.

She took a deep cleansing breath and said, "It's Trent, he has a problem."

Kelsey slid her head phones on Jimmy's ears as she leaned over him and held the wrench on the bolt he was trying to loosen.

Jimmy could feel her breasts snug up against his chest; her lips were no more than inches from his. He was going to tell her; she didn't have to hold the wrench, but hell, he was enjoying the closeness too much to say anything about it. So all he said was, "What happened, Trent?"

"I think I have a bad fuel pump."

"Where are you?" Jimmy asked.

"In Marlette; I'm just outside of town."

"Get yourself a burger, and I'll be there as quick as I can."

Jimmy looked into Kelsey's eyes as he placed the headphones back on her head, and took hold of the wrench.

"You know, I'm getting used to your hair, it wears on a guy."

"What is that supposed to mean?" She looked confused.

"I'm just saying your spiked hair is you. I couldn't picture you wearing your hair any other way."

"You won't have to because this is the way I wear my hair. Are you being sarcastic?" She squinted at him.

"No, I'm not being sarcastic. It's just… Well your hair is you, it has Kelsey written all over it." He chuckled.

He patted her face with his greasy hands, and surprised her by pulling her off the creeper.

Jimmy had her flat on top of him looking into her eyes a moment later. And before they could give what just happened any thought, he pushed the creeper out from underneath the big rig with his feet.

When they came out from under the truck, both his hands were on her bottom. In what seemed to be only a moment later they were lying together in the middle of the garage. Searching each other's eyes for any clue of what the other was thinking.

They were feeling each other's bodies. Lord, how Jimmy wanted to feel her naked flesh against his, although the feeling didn't last long because almost instantly he watched Kelsey nervously struggle up and off the creeper.

All Jimmy did was laugh, because he could tell she was afraid of him. How funny was that, or was it? Maybe she should be afraid of him, because some of the thoughts he was having about her weren't exactly employer-employee thoughts. So he helped her up with his body, and went back to being the employer.

"I'm going to go fix Trent's truck. I'll see you when I get back. I'll have my cell phone with me."

Jimmy was out the door before she could even answer him. He left her thinking what the hell was that all about? And what was all the talk about her hair?

It was raining when Jimmy found Trent's truck on the side of the road. His red pickup pulled in front of the big rig, and he spotted Trent stepping out of the truck, wearing a bright red rain poncho. Jimmy grabbed a bright orange one from his glove box, and slid it over his head. And with a large tool box in one hand, a fuel pump under his other arm. He headed for the big rig and his partner.

Both guys immediately pulled up the fiberglass front end. Jimmy straddling one side of the engine and Trent sat on the other side. They had done all that before they even spoke a word to each other.

Jimmy began taking off the bolts of the old fuel pump when he said, "Couldn't you have broken down somewhere a little dryer?"

"I'll remember that next time," Trent said dryly, and they both smiled.

Jimmy decided it was time to talk to Trent; he needed some advice.

So, he said, "Can I ask you a question, a personal one?"

"Sure," Trent agreed.

How do you know if a girl's right for you?" Jimmy asked as he continued working.

"You just know, or at least I did. The first time I laid eyes on Candy I knew there was something different about her." Trent smiled with the memory.

"What about the other girls? You were known as a real ladies man," Jimmy reminded him.

"You see, that was all a good time. You had sex, and you filed it away as just that," Trent admitted.

"I don't get it; I know it's no surprise to you I've never had a lot of women. There's been a few over the years, but none to really judge by. But Tina, man the girl knows sex, she really knows how to please a man," Jimmy confessed.

The rain was still coming down in sheets when Jimmy looked up at it and Trent.

"If you don't love her, if you don't feel something special with her, if it's good, or not, it's just sex. Don't mistake one for the other. Cause if you love the girl, you can surely have both. Do you love Tina?" Trent asked.

"That's just it. I used to think I did, but the truth is, I feel like she's smothering me. So much so I don't really care about the sex anymore. It's almost as though she turns me off." Jimmy shrugged.

"I've had girls like that in my life. For me it was always the beginning of the end. Unless you're a man whore and sex is all you want in life, I guess the relationship will go on and on. However, if you're a guy who really wants a life long partner, you really have to think about it. Look, Jimmy, I can give you all the advice in the world, but in reality, this is all on you," Trent explained.

"What if you find yourself thinking about someone else?"

"Well, you, my friend, have some decisions to make."

Jimmy knew his problem with Tina was weighing heavy on him, and at the moment, Trent knew it too.

"So, what about that poker game on Saturday? I swear Kelsey's a pro." Trent changed the subject on purpose.

"Yeah, I told her I wanted a chance to get my money back." Jimmy grinned.

"I'm with you." Trent chuckled.

"I've been thinking about Kelsey,"

The sentence was barely out of his mouth when he saw a strange look in Trent's eyes.

Jimmy wasn't ready to discuss Kelsey, at least not yet, and he changed the subject again.

"I mean the poker game at your house, man, the girl can play seven card stud!"

7

Weeks turned into months, and before Kelsey knew it, Thanksgiving had snuck up on her.

She stood in her bedroom looking in the mirror. A different person seemed to reflect back at her. Kelsey was no longer the Goth girl, although her hair and jewelry remained the same, she now wore a beige fitted cashmere sweater tucked into a pair of fitted pinstriped gray slacks. The belted slacks hugged her hips. It was unbelievable how feminine, she'd become. There was even a smile on her face, because Big 4 had given her a life. She had food on her table, and a comfortable furnished apartment, yes, finally a life to look forward to.

It was funny, because thinking of her future brought only one person to mind, Jimmy. The man took to teasing her constantly, even felt obligated to tell her how he thought she should live. There was something sexual going on between them. She smiled at the thought of him patting her bottom, or her face…what was up with that?

Then her expression changed, because he was still seeing Tina, and that thought always brought her back to reality. Jimmy was Tina's, not hers; she would have to face the fact. He cared more for Tina, because they were still together.

She had to let go of any ideas she had about her and Jimmy, they were just friends. So why on earth did she feel the way she did? Why did his stare make her heart pound, and why did the smallest of touches between them make her burn with hot desire for him? Kelsey had to let it all go. He was one of her bosses, and she would just have to treat him like one.

A while later, Kelsey joined her bosses at Trent's house for Thanksgiving dinner. She knocked, walked in the back door and saw Trent and Torrie cutting fresh carrots on the kitchen counter.

She popped one in her mouth and said, "What can I help you with?"

She was a bit surprised when Trent leaned over the counter and whispered loudly, "Please go talk to Candy. I banished her from the kitchen. She was really overdoing it."

"She's due soon, isn't she?" Kelsey asked.

"January 18th and we certainly don't want the baby early," Trent confessed.

Kelsey took the glass of wine Torrie handed her. "Thank you, but where is Bobby?"

"You're replacing him." Torrie giggled.

"Yeah, I'm sure he's had enough of hearing about the baby by now," Trent told her.

"She's going to be a new mom. I'm sure she's just excited," Kelsey soothed.

"You haven't spent much time with, Candy lately, have you?" Torrie smiled.

"Well, no, but she just seems excited, personally I think she goes on like this because she's terrified to have this baby," Kelsey assured them.

"Well, Trent, if that's the case, we'll just have to be patient with her," Torrie said.

"What the hell do you think I've been doing, Torrie? I'm worried to death about all this, but mostly I'm worried about Candy," Trent said, clearly irritated.

Kelsey patted his shoulder. "Don't worry, I'll be happy to talk to your wife. I like Candy. She's one hell of a woman."

"I think she is too." Trent gave her a wink.

Kelsey headed for the living room when she noticed a glazed Bobby listening to Candy fuss about her pregnancy. She tapped Bobby on the shoulder. "Trent and Torrie could use you in the kitchen. I'll sit and visit with Candy."

She couldn't help but smile at Bobby, because he couldn't get out of the living room fast enough. And a moment later, both Candy and Kelsey giggled at the sight.

"Am I that bad, Kelsey?" Candy said with a smile.

"Seems all the guys are not only worried about your pregnancy, but your mental health as well," Kelsey admitted.

"You can't blame me for milking it." Candy shrugged.

Kelsey began to laugh. "I get it. This is all a joke, a way to get a little attention."

She placed her hand over her mouth when Candy put her finger to her lips. "Shush, it gives me lots of company."

Kelsey plopped down next to Candy, who'd propped her legs up on a foot stool positioned in front of the couch.

"Let's talk about something different?" Kelsey suggested.

"Okay, what do you want to know?" Candy asked.

"How did you and Trent meet?"

"I was a waitress in the bar I own." The smile on Candy's face from the memory was unmistakable.

"I didn't know that."

"Yeah. Trent made me quit and drive truck with him. I'm still part owner at the bar, but Trent won't touch my money. He says it's his responsibility to take care of me and my sisters. So the money stays in the bank." Candy shrugged.

"He came into your bar then?"

"Yeah, the first night I met him I beat him up." Candy's happy memory was back on her face.

"What?" The laughter was back in Kelsey's voice.

"Yeah, I didn't take kindly to guys making passes at me. You know working in a bar you get a lot of perverts," Candy explained

"Yeah, you do," Kelsey agreed.

"You've done bar work?" Candy was surprised.

"I've worked in two bars, made good tips too."

"I didn't know you did waitress work."

"I worked my way from New York to Michigan. That's how I bought my car, on tips," Kelsey said proudly.

Before they knew it, both girls were swapping bar stories. They were laughing so hard they had everyone in the living room listening and laughing at their stories too.

It was nearly 5 p.m. when Kelsey saw Benet and Jimmy walk in the back door, open the fridge and grab a beer.

A few moments later they headed into the living room where they caught the tail end of one of Kelsey's bar stories. They entered the room in time to hear the laughter.

"Hi guys, have a seat. Kelsey and Candy are telling some great bar stories." Trent greeted his partners. "Torrie, why don't you and the girls help me set the table."

Kelsey took a sip of wine, and when she looked up she gazed straight into Jimmy's eyes. A long silence fell across the room as Kelsey and Jimmy's eyes locked on one another.

She was so busy looking into Jimmy's eyes she didn't realize Candy was looking from one to the other.

Candy noticed sparks flying between Kelsey and Jimmy. But it was also obvious neither one of them wanted to admit it.

"Did you guys know Kelsey worked in a bar?" Candy broke the silence.

"Doesn't surprise me. I'm sure Kelsey can do anything she puts her mind to. We're just lucky to have her," Benet said first.

"I better go help Trent get the food on the table. We'll talk again soon," Kelsey said as she patted Candy's leg.

"Yeah, seems we have a lot in common," Candy announced.

Candy watched Kelsey pat both Jimmy and Benet's backs as she passed them. "Happy Thanksgiving, guys."

Once she was out of the room a discussion began.

"She's one hell of a girl. One of you two guys should go after her, because she is definitely a prize, and great looking too," Candy said as she looked from one guy man to the other.

"I'm way too old for that pretty little thing. She'd kill me sure as hell." Benet chuckled.

"Well, I guess that leaves you, Jimmy." Candy crossed her arms over her belly.

She stood there staring, and he just smiled at her, and took a big gulp of his beer. However, she wasn't going to let it go.

"Where's your girlfriend? Tina's her name isn't it, Jimmy? You're still seeing her, aren't you?" Candy asked.

"I went over to her parents' house earlier, I ate there with them." He shrugged.

"Oh, so you really don't want to eat here?"

"Listen, Candy, Tina's mother is an awful cook. She can't hold a candle to Trent's cooking. I just ate a little to be polite. I'm going to put the feed bag on here tonight."

A couple hours later, Kelsey stood and helped clear the table, as the men unbuckled their belts. Every one of them seemed to enjoy the feast.

Kelsey set a pile of dishes on the counter next to Torrie; she was washing dishes and Bobby was drying them when she said, "I don't remember the last time I had such a great family Thanksgiving."

"I thought I heard you say you have brothers. Don't they have you over?" Jimmy asked as he stepped into the room and leaned against the door jam.

"We don't see each other. There's been a family problem that's kept us apart." Kelsey shrugged.

"How long has it been?" Bobby asked.

"Six years."

"Can't the problem be fixed?" Jimmy's curiosity was peaked.

"No, Jimmy, someone would have to die first," she said as a matter of fact.

At that moment Kelsey turned when Trent shouted from the dining room. "Come in here everyone, it's time."

Once seated she listened carefully to Benet, who seemed as though he was speaking specifically to her. Come to think of it, all eyes were on her as Benet spoke.

"Kelsey, you've become part of Big 4 trucking. Not just as our dispatcher, but part of the Big 4 family. Because of that, starting next paycheck, you will get one hundred dollars more per week on your check," Benet announced.

All eyes were on her as they watched tears trickle down her face.

"I don't know what to say. Of course the money means a lot to me, but it means even more to me because you consider me more than just an employee, part of Big 4. Thank you." She ran outside to the back screened in porch.

"I think she's happy," Trent said with a shrug.

"Yeah, she's more than happy. She's touched," Candy assured him with a squeeze of her hand.

A half hour later Jimmy volunteered to to bring Kelsey back in for dessert. She'd had enough time to herself.

He stepped out on the porch, quietly closed the door and stepped up behind her. He placed both hands on her shoulders and said, "it's time to come in now, they're serving the pumpkin pie, and I think there's cake too."

He dropped his hands when she turned to him, and he realized she was still drying the tears from her eyes.

"You guys will never know what this means to me," she whispered.

Again he placed his hands gently on her shoulders while he stared longingly into her eyes.

Almost instantly her eyes seemed to call out to him. Jimmy couldn't deny his attraction to her another minute so he pressed his lips gently on hers. Damn, they were soft. The mere touch of their lips was enough to ignite a flame that had been smoldering for months between them.

He couldn't help but take their innocent kiss to a deeper level—couldn't get enough. Their gentle expression of a sweet kiss went wild and before they knew it their passion galloped away from them. It was Jimmy who knew where their little kiss would lead if he didn't stop, and now. So he pulled away and tried to control his breathing, while Kelsey collapsed into his arms.

He rubbed her back and whispered, "Oh, Kelsey."

Jimmy recognized the fact that their single kiss was going to change his life as he knew it. He had been fighting his feelings for Kelsey, now he understood it was no longer possible.

He hugged her hard as he thought, *"Damn it, Kelsey, where do we go from here?"*

He realized their passionate kiss would haunt him. Already he was fighting a burning urge for more, yeah, much more. He was still holding her in his arms when he knew he had to put a stop to this. So he leaned down and whispered in her ear, "We have to go in, they're waiting for us."

He placed an innocent kiss on her nose, saw her straighten up, and smile at him as she stepped out of his warm embrace.

He watched as she looked back at him. Damn, there was longing in her eyes. All he wanted to do was kiss her once more, but dared not.

Jimmy took a deep breath as she walked slowly into the house. He just followed her in silence.

He tried to act as though he hadn't been affected by the heat of her lips. Or the riveting sensation of her breath taking kiss. But hell, he couldn't even stop his hands from shaking, and that's why he placed them in his pockets. Man, he had to do something about this and soon. Because Kelsey was special and he didn't want to play games with her.

However, when they walked into the dining room, he looked as though nothing had happened. Yeah, but he knew down deep inside, Kelsey had captured his heart, and there wasn't a damn thing he could do about it.

Once everyone was seated at the table, dessert was served. They all laughed and talked until nearly 10 p.m.

"I've got to go so I'll see you all on Monday," Jimmy said as he looked down at his watch.

"Don't you want to win some of your money back? Torrie and I are taking all the guys' money tonight. Sure would like yours too." Kelsey grinned.

"How about I take a rain check. There's something I have to do tonight." With a wink in Kelsey's direction, he said his good-byes and off he went.

While Thanksgiving dinner was being transformed into a card game. Kelsey made her way to the kitchen where she poured herself a glass of wine.

A moment later Candy came in. "You like him, Jimmy that is?"

"Yes, I do, but it doesn't matter. Tina has a tight grip on him, and I don't think he wants to break it."

"Don't give up. He just may surprise you." Candy hugged her.

All Kelsey tried to do was hold back the tears, but she knew she couldn't hide the hurt in her eyes.

"Okay, let's go win all the guys' money." It was obvious Candy was trying to change the subject.

"You know something, Candy, taking the guys' money always seems to make me feel better." Kelsey grinned. And both girls left the room, laughing.

Before long Torrie came into the kitchen with Bobby at her heals.

"Bobby, I'm capable of making my own turkey sandwich."

"Oh, I believe you are. I just thought I could talk you into making one for me too." He grinned at her.

Torrie began making the sandwiches as Bobby leaned against the counter, watching, his arms folded across his chest.

"So, when is school going to be done?" he asked.

She placed the turkey on the bread as she said, "Another four years."

"You'll be gone even more than you are now, won't you?"

"Why do you ask? Is there something you want to tell me?" She turned and faced him.

Torrie had been fighting her feelings where Bobby was concerned for a very long time now. It seemed whenever she thought of a husband and family she always thought of him.

She stared right into his eyes because she was searching for an answer only he could give her.

Suddenly he answered her question with another. "Is there something you want to tell me?"

Torrie hoped he would tell her how much she was loved. But she also feared he didn't care for her, at least not like she cared for him.

She didn't know how Bobby felt, to be honest, since he never shared his feelings. So she had no idea, which meant, again, they were at a stalemate.

So with a deep breath, Torrie cut the sandwich in half on the plate and handed it to him. She was staring into his eyes when she asked again, "You're sure there isn't anything you want to say to me, Bobby?"

"No, Torrie, at least not now," he said with disappointment in his voice.

She shook her head at him, and they both headed for the dinning room and the card game.

Ten miles away, Jimmy stood knocking on Tina's door. He was taken aback when she answered the door in a black satin teddy, one of her hands was high on the door jamb, the other on her hip. He watched her throw her head back and her hair whipped around her shoulders, and she gave him an alluring smile. Jimmy understood exactly what she wanted from him.

"I knew you'd come tonight, even though you said you wouldn't see me until tomorrow. I knew you would want me." Her voice dripped with seduction.

Jimmy stepped in and closed the door behind him. He was trying to ignore her sexual advances so he sat at the dining room table. He could see Tina wasn't letting this go. He thought she seemed to slither provocatively into his lap.

A moment later his chest grew warm from her fingers as they slid ever so slowly up and down his shirt. There was no doubt she was tempting him with all her womanly wilds.

"I always knew what my baby wanted and needed." The sensation of her hot breath in his ear had him trying to think straight.

He immediately pulled away when she placed his hand on the satin material which covered her breasts. Then he froze when she placed his other hand on her upper bare thigh.

All he said was, "Can you and I just talk, Tina?"

"I guess we could talk before we hit the sheets. What is it you want to talk about?" She sounded irritated.

"I'd like to see if we have other things in common," he explained.

"What do you mean?"

"Look, Tina, all you and I do is have sex."

"I know, and great sex it is." She gave him a wink and a smile.

"Yes, Tina, the sex between us is good, but you need more in a relationship, you know, and so do I. What do we have in common? Do we like the same games?" He tried to encourage her to share.

"Of course we do, and the game is love." She grinned devilishly.

"You see, there you go again, I mean other than sex. I don't even know your favorite color, or your favorite flower. Damn it, Tina, I don't know anything about you!" He let his frustration show.

"Don't get so upset, honey. What's between us works. If it's not broken, don't fix it!" She raised an eyebrow at him.

Suddenly he was almost knocked off the chair when she planted a deep tongue sweeping kiss in his mouth.

Jimmy pulled away, took hold of both her arms and looked into her eyes. "Can't we just talk? We've been together for a while now. I'd like to make this work with you, please, but we have to talk."

"I think action speaks louder than word." She gave him a bare shouldered shrug meant to entice.

Again he had to pull away from her advances. "Tina, talk to me. What sort of life do you want? Do you like children?"

"You know, Jimmy, children take up a lot of time. If we have children there won't be any time for you and me. For going out and doing what we love to do, if you know what I mean. She began nibbling his neck.

All of a sudden he realized she was unbuckling his belt and unzipping his pants, and she didn't stop until she felt his urgency.

He knew she was gloating at the situation. Jimmy also figured Tina assumed she could keep him with sex. And at that moment, he didn't even care.

So, he took her fast and furiously on the floor, right there by the dining room table. At this point it was all about giving his body what he wanted, and that's exactly what he did without a second thought. It was wham, bam, not even a thank you, ma'am.

When it was over, he lay next to her on the floor, buckling his pants. And before long he took to his feet, just as Tina sat up on the floor half undressed, and staring at him.

"What are you doing, Jimmy?"

"I'm going home."

"What…? You just got here, and we have all night to make love." She sounded like she purred.

"No Tina, I don't think so. I was hoping to get to know you better, have a relationship with you. Seems, you don't want to connect in any way. All you want is sex. I just don't see how this can work." He shook his head at her.

"Jimmy, we can try." She placed her hand on his arm.

"Tina, I've had a great time with you. We've had lots of laughs, but you and I want different things. You want sex; I want someone to have a relationship with. You and I are from two different worlds."

Jimmy hugged her, and placed a sweet kiss on her forehead.

"It's been fun, take care." Without another word he went out the door, closing it behind him.

Once he was in his truck, he sat there running his fingers through his short hair. Jimmy felt he needed to give Tina a chance, even though things hadn't been working between them for a long time. But things turned out just as he thought they would. Tina only wanted what Tina wanted, and that wasn't working for him any longer. It was sad, and one hell of a tangled mess, but a fact just the same.

Jimmy was looking for a life with someone, a relationship and love, just like Trent and Candy had. And no matter who it turned out to be, he wouldn't settle for less.

Tina sat at her dining room table, crying. How could she have lost him? She did everything a man would want. Then she stared off, and cried out loud, "Damn, Kelsey." Everything went sour when she was hired. The girl stole her man, and she wasn't going to let her get away with it.

Tina swore right there and then she would figure a way to make Kelsey pay. Once she was out of the picture, Jimmy would come crawling back to her.

She smiled at the thought of Jimmy begging her for sex. She would make him grovel, just for a short time, but she would take him back. Yes, Kelsey would pay; she just had to figure out how.

8

Jimmy walked into the Big 4 Trucking office Monday morning, a smile on his face and a spring in his step. He saw Bobby sitting at his desk, staring at some paperwork. Kelsey stood filing at the file cabinet. He thought she looked great. She appeared to have a new outfit on, or at least he hadn't seen it before. And man, did it look good on her; it showed off her great little figure. So he whistled, and Kelsey turned and smiled.

"New outfit?" Jimmy asked.

"Yeah, Trent, Benet and Bobby got it for me," she said proudly.

"We sure did. Kelsey and Torrie took every penny we had on Thanksgiving. Hell, Torrie even got my watch," Bobby complained.

Jimmy began to chuckle. "Boy, am I glad I left when I did. I probably would have lost my shirt."

"Why did you leave?" Kelsey asked.

"I had something I had to take care of," he said nonchalantly.

"Well, did you?" She raised an eyebrow.

"Yep, I did."

"Whatever it was seems it's made you happy. In fact, I've never seen you this happy on a Monday since I started working here."

"It took me a while to find out what I wanted, and now that I have, life's a better place."

Jimmy didn't speak any more about it, he just poured himself a cup of coffee and with a grin in Kelsey's direction, he went into the garage.

When he closed the door, she stood staring at it.

"What are you thinking about?" Bobby asked.

"I'm thinking about the change in Jimmy. He's like a different guy," she said as she continued to stare.

The phrase was no sooner spoken when Tina stormed in the front door, slamming it behind her.

"Where is he?" Tina caught Kelsey off guard.

"Excuse me?" she asked.

"Where is Jimmy, and don't act so innocent. You know he called it off between us," Tina shouted.

"I don't know what you're talking about. Jimmy hasn't said anything to us, so I don't have a clue what's going on between you two," Kelsey blurted out.

"You can drop the act. I know he dumped me for you," Tina insisted.

"Look, Tina, we were both surprised by your statement. Kelsey's right. Jimmy hasn't said anything to anyone. And if you think Jimmy would talk to us about his relationship with you, then you don't know him very well. Jimmy, or anyone of us here at Big 4, keep our personal life, personal. We don't kiss and tell," Bobby informed her from his desk.

Tina turned her back on Bobby, ignored him and stormed into the garage.

"I don't know what I ever did to Tina to make her hate me so much." Kelsey gave Bobby a look of confusion.

"She needs someone to blame for her troubles, Kelsey. At least now we know why the change in Jimmy," Bobby told her and she went back to her filing.

Tina came into the garage just as Jimmy was sliding his last arm into his overhauls and she slammed the door behind her.

"Tina?" He looked surprised.

"Yeah, it's me. We have to talk."

"Look, Tina, there's nothing to talk about. It's over between us," he said calmly.

Tina stood in front of Jimmy and placed both her arms around his neck. "I think we should talk about this. You know we have lots of fun together. You're just a little confused by that Kelsey girl. She's clouded your feelings for me. I'm not naïve, Jimmy. I know men are attracted by something new, different, however, I'm telling you, she won't be as good to you as I am."

She ran her fingers over the buttons of his shirt under the open overhauls and whispered, "She won't understand what it is you need like I will. You know I'm telling the truth, I understand how you like your love making, I can please you. Honestly I can."

She watched as Jimmy took hold of her hands that were now unbuttoning his shirt, and he looked her straight in the eyes. If she didn't know better she would have sworn the look he gave her was as cold as ice.

"First of all, Tina, Kelsey has nothing to do with us. She just works here. She's a nice girl, a good worker, that's all I care about. And we did have fun together, the sex was good, but it ended there. You and I are looking for two different things. You're looking for a good time, a sex partner, a possession. I'm looking for a relationship, a partner in life. Tina, I would cramp your style, and you know it."

Tears filled her eyes. "I can be whatever you want me to be, Jimmy. I don't want to lose you, or what we had together." She tried to convince him.

"You're making this harder than it has to be. You don't need me. There are lots of guys out there who would love to have a woman like you." He shook his head at her.

Tina looked away from him and stared off for a moment, until suddenly she headed for the door. Yet, before her hand took hold of the door knob she turned to him.

"You see, Jimmy, there's just one problem, I'm in love with you, and one day you're going to realize you love me too."

And out the door she went, only to run right into Kelsey, who was carrying a pile of contracts to file. Tina gave her a push.

The files went flying out of Kelsey's hands. Tina saw Kelsey turn on her with murderess eyes.

"Have I wronged you in another life? What the hell is your problem?" Kelsey raised her voice.

Tina got right in Kelsey's face and hollered, "You're my problem!"

At that point she just walked over the contracts on the floor and hurried out the door.

Kelsey took off after her, but before she could take hold of the glass door handle, Bobby caught her attention.

"Let it go, Kelsey. She's a bitch and can't help it," Bobby said as he stepped in front of her and took hold of her shoulders.

"I'm telling you, Bobby, I can't be held responsible for what I do to her the next time I see her. I've taken her crap for the last time!" Kelsey shouted.

"I understand how you feel, but this is an office. Our place of business, so just let it go."

At that point she was beginning to calm down, so she nodded at Bobby. He let go of her, and with a shake of her head, she took to her knees on the floor where she began picking up the files.

She didn't see Jimmy enter the office until he said, "What happened here?"

Kelsey never looked up from her task when she said, "Your girlfriend is what happened!"

Before she knew it, Jimmy was down on his knees helping her with the files.

"What are you talking about?" Jimmy asked.

Kelsey glanced over and saw Bobby on his knees on the other side of her picking up files too.

"I think Tina was a little angry and kind of took it out on Kelsey and these files," Bobby explained.

"Why would she do something like that?" Jimmy was confused.

Kelsey stared at him. "Are you in denial, or what? If she could have killed me, she would have, but seeing she couldn't she took it out on these files." She continued staring at Jimmy as he sat back on his heels.

"So, she really did this?"

"I've tried to stay out of your personal affairs, Jimmy, but if Tina can't be civil to Kelsey, better she doesn't come here. This is a place of business." Bobby shook his head.

"I'm sorry, Kelsey, that somehow you got caught in the middle of all of this. I'm sure she won't come by anymore. I made it perfectly clear to her things between us are over," Jimmy assured her.

Kelsey was staring at the contracts as she tried to put them back together. "Whatever you told her, just made her madder, you know."

"Again, I'm sorry. For some ungodly reason she thinks you're the reason I called our relationship off. I told her it had nothing to do with you, and our break-up had been coming for a long time now."

"Well, by the looks of what she did here, she doesn't believe a word you said." She shook her head.

"What made you change your mind about her?" Bobby asked.

Jimmy shrugged. "She's just not the one, Tina and I had fun, a good time. I'll never forget her for what we had, but she's just not the girl I want to spend the rest of my life with."

"I'm sorry, Jimmy. I'm sorry because I can't let her walk all over me, just because you feel sorry about dumping her. I've been pushed around a lot in my life. I can't and won't let Tina take her anger out on me. So don't be surprised if I punch her lights out next time I see her!" Kelsey raised her voice.

"I promise you won't see her anymore. It's over. She just needs a few days to accept it." Jimmy shrugged.

"Let's hope so, because she's really pissing me off," Kelsey said with an attitude.

Two weeks had gone by when Kelsey realized there hadn't been any word from Tina. She was beginning to believe Jimmy was right about the girl. Time would tell.

It was a late Friday afternoon, nearly a month later, when Jimmy realized it was time for Kelsey to head home. There were only two people left in the Big 4 office; Jimmy and Kelsey.

"Good night, Jimmy, see you on Monday," Kelsey said.

He walked into the office wiping his hands on a shop rag and gave her a smile. "Yeah, have a great weekend."

"Thanks, you too," she said on her way out the door.

Jimmy watched her leave when he noticed snow was falling in large flakes on the ground. The pavement was covering quickly.

He began to worry when he saw Kelsey head for her car. She unlocked the door and put the key in the ignition, and he heard it crank and crank, but not start.

A few moments later he watched her get out of the car with a slam of the door. He smiled because she opened the hood and stared down at the engine, as if she had any idea what she was looking at.

The grin on Jimmy's face was big as he saw her jiggle the battery cables, hit the alternator with her fist, and curse.

"It's the starter, Kelsey, can't you hear the clicking?" he yelled from the office door as he locked it, and slid his jacket on.

He was still grinning when he approached her and the car.

"Oh, damn it, Jimmy, I'm tired and cold, I just want to go home," she whined.

Without a word, he reached into the car and yanked the keys out of the ignition, and her purse off the seat. He locked the door with her keys. "I'll take you home and I'll order a starter in the morning."

"I can't ask you to do that," she argued.

"You didn't ask, I volunteered. Now c'mon, I'll drive you home."

Jimmy saw her take a deep breath and he smiled and headed for his bright red truck. She seemed to drag her body behind him.

He was starting the truck when she slid into the passenger seat, and sat there like a lump. It wasn't long before Jimmy looked the exact same way she did because he was waiting for Kelsey to notice they were still stopped at the sign at the end of Big 4s driveway. He looked over at her and she glanced at Jimmy, who was staring at her, with a wide grin.

"What?" she asked.

"You know, Kelsey, I consider myself a fairly smart guy. However, I don't happen to have osmosis. I can't drive you home if you don't tell me where you live."

Jimmy knew the exact moment she got it because she looked up and saw where they were, and Kelsey couldn't help but shake her head at her silliness.

"I have a lower flat down here on Main Street in town. I'll show you."

He headed out of the driveway as he said, "It's pretty cool you're so close to work."

"I took it because it was a pretty big flat, but mostly because the price was right."

"Me, Benet and Bobby share an old farm house. We bought it when we moved the business here a few years ago. It's worked out real well for us."

Jimmy cleared his throat, because he knew the question he was about to ask was personal, but he had to ask it. "Do you have a boyfriend here in town?"

"No, there really hasn't been time in my life for men. I work a lot of hours. You know that, Jimmy, since you're one of my bosses for heaven sakes." She shook her head.

"Yeah, you do work a lot of hours, but it doesn't mean you don't have someone. You're a good looking woman, Kelsey. I'd think you'd be fighting the guys off with a stick."

"The only guys I ever fought off were the drunks at the bars I worked at. No, Jimmy, there is no one interested in me. There it is right there, go around back." She pointed.

Jimmy pulled around the building and parked right by the back door. When he put the truck in park he looked over at her and said, "When are we going to stop playing cat and mouse, Kelsey? I like you, I like you a lot."

"Look, Jimmy, you're my boss, and then there's the Tina thing."

"There's no Tina thing, Kelsey, and as far as me being your boss, I could give the responsibility fully to Bobby. We can make him your only boss, If it will make you happy? So there, Kelsey, problem solved."

A moment later he noticed she sat back against the truck door and gave him her full attention.

"You're sure this thing between you and Tina is over?" she asked.

He leaned against his door and grinned at her. "Aren't you going to ask me in? Don't you think it would be better to talk inside?"

"Are you hungry?"

"Please, I'm always hungry," he joked.

He was pleased with himself when Kelsey dug deep into her purse and pulled her keys out.

"I hope you like stew. I've had it in the slow cooker all day."

Jimmy rubbed his hands together. "Home made stew, damn!" He smiled from ear to ear.

"Don't praise it until you've tasted it." She giggled.

Jimmy stepped into a different world when Kelsey opened the door. It was a place he wouldn't have ever known was hers. She placed her purse and keys on the table, and when she turned to him he was staring at the kitchen.

"Is something wrong?" she said seriously.

"No, not at all, I just didn't picture you being well…domestic."

"Why not?" she asked.

"Well, your spiked hair. Your Goth flare, but this room screams home and comfort."

"I like some Goth style, but not all. I think we are all influenced by what makes us happy. I also believe people do what makes them content, and I'm no exception. Now c'mon and sit right here at the table while I put some rolls in the oven." She beamed up at him.

He sat down as he kept an eye on her. She hung up her coat, took his and went right to work, all while Jimmy took in his surroundings.

A moment later her voice pulled him out of his thoughts.

"Relax, make yourself comfortable, Jimmy."

Then without warning he pulled her into his lap, and she let out a scream. He chuckled in her ear.

"You scared me Jimmy," she said with her hand on her heart.

"I didn't mean to frighten you," he whispered.

At that moment he gazed deeply into her eyes. His heart started pounding and heat surged through his veins. So what happened next was almost out of his control.

Jimmy leaned closer and closer until their lips were only a whisper away. Her eyes seemed soft and warm, and her lips were almost calling out to him to be kissed. Damn, before he could stop himself his mouth took hers, and their kiss seemed to explode with heat that seared their lips.

He was encouraged when she wrapped her arms around his neck and cuddled in close. So close, he could feel her breasts tight up against his chest.

Jimmy couldn't control his body from reacting. Hell, her mouth was so inviting and she smelled wonderful, and his hands began to shake.

He didn't want this beautiful moment to end, and by the way Kelsey was kissing him back, he'd wager she felt the same way. Yet he also knew he had to end this fiery kiss before it consumed them both, and a moment later he did.

They sat staring into each other's eyes, their lips were still so close the kiss could easily happen again.

"I hope you don't mind. I was just doing what you said, making myself at home?" He gave her a crooked smile.

"I have to check the rolls," Kelsey said as she rose from his lap and swallowed hard.

Jimmy wanted to laugh at her complete change of subject, although he didn't. He wasn't going to push his luck. He knew he was moving a little fast but hell, it seemed as though he'd been interested in her for a long while.

That semi Goth look of hers always had him staring at her when she climbed up on a big rig, or rolled underneath it. His heart would skip a beat at the sight of her sparkling eyes and smiling face.

And to be perfectly honest, his relationship with Tina had been over a long time ago. Like the song says, "All that was happening was a long goodbye."

A deep breath escaped his lungs because he'd kind of taken advantage of the situation. He felt a little bad about it, but now it was time to see where it led him.

Jimmy took a big whiff of the steaming bowl of stew Kelsey placed in front of him. It smelled wonderful. He saw her place one across from him, a baking dish of rolls, and a little plate with butter was set right in the middle of the table. Then he smiled when she sat across from him, her face was blushing red.

"This smells great," Jimmy said.

"Don't smell it, eat it, I make a mean pot of stew, at least I think I do."

They both dug into the stew at the same time. Jimmy couldn't help, but look ever so pleased with the first bite. It wasn't long before he was asking for seconds. Kelsey jumped up at his request, happy to oblige.

Jimmy had just gotten his second helping and she sat back down when he realized the subject had turned to Tina once more.

"Can I ask you a personal question?" she said as she slid her fingers through the hair at her temples.

"Sure, what do you want to know?" he asked as he placed another bite of stew in his mouth.

"Why did you break up with Tina? I thought you were head over heals for her?" she said as she stared into the half eaten bowl of stew.

"It took me some time to realize we wanted different things out of life. I wanted to talk more to find out what we have in common but she didn't want to." He shrugged.

Jimmy saw her nod, as if she understood.

A moment later out of the blue, he said, "May I ask you a personal question?"

"Sure." She gave him her full attention.

"Why bring up, Tina, when I just told you I'm interested in you?"

"Because I don't want to be anyone's rebound girl," she blurted out.

Jimmy took her hand in his across the table. "I assure you, my interest in you is not of a rebound nature. Because what Tina and I had was more… more…"

"Of a sexual nature," she filled in the words for him.

He gave her a surprised look. "How did you…?

"For God sakes, Jimmy, it was written all over you and her. The way you looked at each other, the way she touched you. Even a girl with limited experience like me could see that!"

Jimmy took a deep breath. "Look, Kelsey, I'd rather not even talk about Tina. It's over, can't we just leave it?"

"I guess it's not really any of my business anyway."

"Now, can we focus on each other?" He wanted to change the subject.

She nodded.

"Good, now tell me about yourself," he asked.

"There's really not much to tell. I was born and raised in the city. My mother died from cancer when I was fifteen. After she was gone, my father couldn't go on; he started taking drugs." Kelsey shrugged. "Thank God we were all old enough to take care of ourselves when he died from a drug overdose."

"Did he do drugs before your mom died?" Jimmy asked.

"All of us kids knew he liked his weed and booze. However, none of us would have ever thought he'd turn to the serious stuff so quickly. The whole drug thing scared me so much, I swore I'd never even take an aspirin unless I needed it."

Jimmy took another bite of the delicious stew as he stared off in silence.

"This whole drug thing turns you off to me, doesn't it?" Kelsey asked.

Jimmy sat back in his chair, swallowed his food, looked right into her eyes and answered her questions. "Do you take drugs?"

"I told you, I don't even take an aspirin unless I really need it."

"Then this drug thing has nothing whatsoever to do with us. We can't help what goes on in our families. In my family it was alcohol, in yours it's drugs. As long as we don't go down the same road, make their mistakes, I figure we'll be fine. You and I don't have to live their lives. Our lives are what we make of it."

Kelsey nodded her head. Because he was right, she felt the exact same way about the whole thing. However, at that moment, she decided not to tell him about her brother, Josh, at least not until she knew him better.

So she changed the subject "Would you like to see the rest of my flat?"

"Yes, I would love to see your house."

Kelsey stood and headed out of the kitchen, Jimmy at her heals. They walked through a comfortably decorated living room and into a hallway where she opened a door and revealed her bedroom.

Although the room was neatly kept with a colorful quilt, pillowcases and dust ruffle on the bed, all Jimmy imagined was Kelsey laying there at night, waiting for him. He took a deep breath because he found himself staring at Kelsey's body, trying to undress her with his eyes.

She noticed Jimmy's stare, and said, looking down at her blouse. "Is my shirt unbuttoned?"

"No. I was just thinking of something," he said quickly.

She closed the bedroom door and opened another one across the hall where a large sewing machine sat near the window. Bright colored material lay on it, as if she'd been working on something.

"You sew?" Jimmy asked.

"Yes, I find it calming. You seemed surprised.

"You just… I mean… I didn't think you were the domestic type."

"Why?" she asked curiously.

"It's just you always appear to be Goth. Look at your spiked hair. You just don't fit into this place."

"I guess I can understand, still you shouldn't judge a book by its cover," she teased.

"You're proof of that, Kelsey."

In the next instant she led him into the living room where they sat on the couch. Kelsey folded her hands nervously in her lap and Jimmy smiled at the telling action.

"Well, Kelsey, I love it, your home that is. It gave me a special insight into the real Kelsey, not the somewhat Goth girl, but you."

She smiled up at him, and with both his thumbs he wiped off her dark blue lipstick.

"Sorry girl, now that I know you better, this stuff doesn't fit you." Slowly, he leaned in close.

Their eyes met and she noticed he gave her a wicked sort of grin. Then she closed her eyes when he captured her lips. The kiss was gentle, yet consuming. She wouldn't mind if he stoked her fire like he was doing all night long. No, she wouldn't mind one bit.

Her eyes were still closed when he pulled away, and by God she was in a trance. Kelsey hoped she had a look of contentment on her face, because content was how she felt. And before she knew it he stole another kiss, but this time he pulled her close.

Kelsey knew she wanted to give him back everything he was giving her, until she came to her senses and pulled away. She knew if she didn't, he could take her right there on the couch and God help her she'd let him.

"What's wrong, Kelsey?"

"Nothing."

"Then why did you…?" He searched her eyes.

She slid her fingers gently over his lips as she spoke in a soft whisper. "Too fast, Jimmy, we're going too fast. I'm not a girl of vast experience so there's a lot to think about here. I like you, really I do, maybe even more than I should, but you've just broken up with your girlfriend and I work for you."

"I thought we discussed all of this?"

"We did, still I need to give this lots of thought. I can't just jump into bed with you because you say you're interested in me."

"Did I ask you to go to bed with me?" He looked dead serious.

"You know where those kisses will land us, and if you keep kissing me like this, I'll go willingly. I don't want to be a one night stand," she argued.

"You would not be a one night stand."

"Maybe not, but I have to know in my heart that you and I are going somewhere, and not just to bed."

"Alright, we'll do it your way."

She smiled when Jimmy held her cheeks in his hands. She watched him place a sweet kiss on her lips, only to pull away and whisper, "Good night, Kelsey."

A moment later she was pulled up out of the couch with him as he said, "Walk me to the door, okay?"

She nodded and he took hold of her hand as they went to the back door. She took his coat from the hook and held it out for him. He slid his arms in, and she turned him around and buttoned his coat. She buttoned the last button at his throat and gave it a little pat, and she saw Jimmy smiling down at her.

"Will I be warm enough?" His voice bordered on laughter.

She patted the button on his chest and said, "Yes, now you will be."

Again she found herself in his arms.

"Good night, Kelsey, and before you go to sleep tonight give me a thought, will you?"

"Oh, I'll be giving you lots of thought," she assured him.

"Thanks for dinner and especially for those great kisses." He chuckled.

"You may have one more," she said with a nod.

"Oh I can, can I?"

She stood there in his arms, eyes closed, waiting for her good night kiss. However, Jimmy was so tickled by her, he just kissed the tip of her nose.

"Until next time, Kelsey, good night."

The disappointment on her face was evident, and Jimmy laughed out the door and all the way to his truck.

Kelsey closed the door and leaned against it. There was a sigh on her lips, because he was really leaving her with a lot to think about.

She'd liked him since the first time she saw him at Big 4. And when he kissed her on Thanksgiving, she thought she'd never stop feeling his breath taking kiss on her lips. Yet to find out he actually liked her too, caught her off guard. Heaven help her; she really did have a lot to think about.

A moment later she headed for the front window and watched Jimmy drive away. Again Kelsey sighed; she needed to get herself together. It was time to clean up the kitchen and go to bed. That would be the time to give what just happened between her and Jimmy some thought.

She had the kitchen sparkling clean when she heard a knock at the back door. Kelsey never gave it a second thought, she knew it was Jimmy. He must have forgotten something. With a glance around the room, she went to the door, opened it with the biggest smile for Jimmy, and laughed when she said, "What did you forget?"

Suddenly her expression changed from one of complete pleasure to fear. And she began to back away from the terrifying image before her. The snicker on her brother's face made her stomach lurch.

"Where you goin', Kelsey? Don't you want to give your brother a warm welcome? It's been a long time, sister. Give your brother a hug."

All Kelsey did was shake her head slowly at him as she continued to back away.

"Oh, c'mon, Kelsey. We're family,"

Instantly she noticed he spotted the open container of still warm stew on the table and went right to it.

"Now, let's see, you always kept the silverware on the right of the sink, lets see if you've changed." He opened the drawer and saw the silverware neatly stacked there. A deep laugh filled the air.

"Same old Kelsey. I bet you even have a tidy little sum of money in the bank too. You were always such a little saver."

"How'd you find me Josh?" Her voice cracked.

"A little birdie told me," he said as he dug into the stew.

"Well, you're not welcome here. I gave you more money than I should have. I've a life here, and a good one, please don't ruin this for me," she begged.

"Hell, all I want is your money and I'll leave you the hell alone!"

"Yeah, until the money runs out. No, I'm done working for you. Do you hear me… I'm finished!"

She cringed when Josh glared at her as he threw the almost empty container across the room.

"You'll do what I tell you, or I'll beat the hell out of you, and take your money anyway. If I remember correctly, you always kept money in the house, and lots of it."

"I told you Josh, I'm done!"

Kelsey watched Josh walk slowly across the room to her, then he grabbed both her arms, and she winced.

"Don't you remember the last beating I gave you for trying to hide money from me?" he said in a near shout.

She stared into his angry black eyes with hatred as she said, "Oh, I haven't forgotten. You almost killed me the last time. And you'll have to kill me now, because there's no way in hell I'll give you a dime of my money, not one damn dime."

She staggered back when he pulled back his hand and with all his strength he slapped her.

"You will give me that money, or I will kill you. I'm not above doing what I need to for money." He slapped her in the face again.

Pain shot through her cheek-bones and burned like a hot poker into her eye.

Kelsey gave him an icy cold stare. There were no tears in her eyes. She refused to let him know how bad his slap hurt.

There was no doubt in her mind, he would probably kill her this time, and as God as her witness, still she refused to give him any joy in it.

Kelsey understood Josh loved to inflict pain, it made him feel powerful. No, she wouldn't cry, nor would she scream, there was only a silent prayer it would be over quickly, until it came, a punch she never saw coming. Kelsey staggered back. Because a moment later she knew he broke her nose. Blood ran down her lips and the swelling seemed to throb through her whole face. All she wanted to do was scream with pain, yet she refused to even whimper.

"Damn it, Kelsey, if you tell me where the money is I'll stop, I swear."

The hateful stare she gave him made him let go of her arm. Except Kelsey couldn't let it go; she had to confront him.

"Your promises aren't worth anything, Josh."

Kelsey watched the rage in her brother's eyes once more as he threw a punch that landed her half on the couch and half on the floor in the other room She no sooner caught her breath from the fierce blow of his fist, when she saw him come after her again.

She felt as though she was fading away when he lifted her body up by her sweater. But, just when she thought there was nothing she could do about what was going to happen to her next, her brother pulled back his fist to punish her once more.

Kelsey caught a glimpse of someone she thought looked like Jimmy, the man was filling the open back door. Although, before Josh noticed him, his punch landed in Kelsey's face once more.

Jimmy's fury rose like fire through his body. He'd never experienced anger like this before, so without even thinking, he found himself in the living room throwing Josh back into the kitchen. Where his head hit the stove and he laid there knocked out cold. Seeing this, Jimmy left Josh so he could help Kelsey, who now lay on the floor in a heap.

Jimmy lifted her up on the couch and laid her down. Kelsey took hold of his hand. "Oh, thank you for coming back, he would have killed me if you hadn't."

"Who is he and what does he want?" Jimmy raised his voice.

"He's my brother."

"Your brother…? He was trying to kill you." Jimmy couldn't believe it.

"He would have too, if it wasn't for you," she cried.

"I'm calling the police!"

Jimmy was dialing 911 when he noticed Josh. He must have heard the word police because he hurried out the back door before he could catch him. Jimmy looked over at Kelsey. "I'm calling them anyway."

"Jimmy, he's gone, I don't want to answer a hundred questions right now, not like this."

He hit a button on the phone to end the call, went into the kitchen and closed the back door.

Then he went through every drawer looking for anything he could find to help Kelsey.

A few moments later he was taking care of her face. Once he had her cleaned up, he went back into the kitchen and wrapped ice cubes in a kitchen towel.

He had her sitting up on the couch as he held the home made ice pack on her face.

"So, are you going to tell me why the hell your brother was trying to beat you to death?" he said with anger in his voice.

Jimmy held the ice pack on her eye when she answered him. "Like my father, he has problems with drugs."

"He thought you'd have drugs?"

"He knows I don't do drugs. But he does know I work, so he comes to me looking for money," she explained.

"And you took a beating rather than give him the money?" He shook his head at her.

"Jimmy, if I gave him money, he would keep coming back for more. I used to work as a dispatcher in the city. When he lived with me, I got beat almost every week because all he wanted was my money. I was lucky if I could pay the rent before he got his hands on it, and food, forget it. I had to beg him for my own hard earned money for some bread and peanut butter just to survive. No, I won't give him my money anymore." She sounded determined.

"You know you could have gone to the police with this? You could get an injunction against him," Jimmy informed her.

"Believe me, Josh doesn't play by the rules. He would have found a way to get to me and my money. The law means nothing to him." Tears ran down her cheek.

The ice pack was on her face. When Jimmy took it off he placed it on her swollen eye.

"Maybe I should take you to the hospital."

"Are you kidding? You did a great job patching me up." Kelsey gave him a half smile through her swollen lips.

"Can you walk?" Jimmy asked as he took a deep breath.

"I think so," she said softly.

Jimmy helped her up, placed his arm around her waist and guided her across the room to her bedroom where he sat her gently on the bed.

"What do you wear to bed?" he inquired.

"Excuse me?" She was taken back.

"Kelsey, I want you to get some rest. I'm going to give you some aspirins and get you into bed."

"In the top drawer, you'll see some pajamas folded there." She pointed him in the right direction.

He opened the drawer and saw everything folded neatly in place. Boy, this little Goth girl was a constant surprise to him.

When he turned to her he handed her a pair of pajamas. "Do you need help?"

"No, I can do it, thank you."

He gave her a gentle smile, closed the door behind him, and left her to it.

Kelsey was undressing as she thought about her brother. She knew she hadn't seen the last of him. Yes, he'd figured out there was money, no doubt in her mind he'd come to that conclusion, quickly. And nothing would keep him from having it, not even her life. Running again, and far, was her only option.

As she carefully slid the top of her pajamas over her head, her thoughts went to Jimmy. She liked him, really liked him. Not only would she have to run from Josh, but she would have to walk away from Jimmy and Big 4 too. Hell, why did Josh have to turn up now. Damn him, and damn my father for getting him into such a horrible habit.

Kelsey's body screamed with pain as she slowly slid into bed. Once under the covers, she heard the bedroom door open. There she saw Jimmy in the doorway with a steaming cup of tea in his hand.

"This will make you feel better," he said.

She took a big sip of the tea and gave her head a shake. "This has liquor in it, and boy is it strong."

"It will help you rest, Kelsey." He chuckled. "I've been carrying around this unopened bottle of whiskey in my truck. It was for one of our suppliers, a Christmas gift. Haven't seen him, so I thought you could sure use it more than him right now." He sat down on the edge of the bed next to her.

"You know I'll have to leave now?"

"And why is that?" he asked with seriousness.

"Because Josh won't stop until he either has all my money, or I'm dead. That's the way he is."

"Listen, how long have you been running from him?" he said as he looked down on her black polished nails.

"Five, maybe six years." She shrugged.

"Do you want to live in fear of him, or do we want to do something about it?"

"What can I do?" Her eyes welled up with tears.

"Get the police involved, and you're not alone anymore. You have me, and Big 4 behind you now."

"You're all great guys, but I can't ask you to fight my battles for me," she said as a tear slid down her cheek.

"You didn't, I offered. Tonight we start by me spending the night."

Her eyes opened wide, and he grinned.

"I'll sleep on the couch," he assured her.

"Oh..."

Kelsey smiled slightly when he patted her hand and stood to do just that, except when he reached for the door knob, Kelsey asked, "Why did you come back?"

She watched him pull her wallet out of his back pocket and show it to her.

"When I stopped at the stop light up the street it slid across the seat, and hit me in the thigh. I figured you'd need your wallet come morning, so I brought it back."

"Well, whatever the reason, I owe you big time."

"Anything for you, sweet thing." He winked at her.

Jimmy smiled and gently closed the door behind him. He was thinking how he didn't tell her the whole truth about the wallet, because after it hit his thigh, he thought it was the perfect reason to get a few more kisses out of her, and now, he didn't care what the reason, he was just glad he came back. If he hadn't showed up when he did, Kelsey would have surely been beaten much worse, maybe even killed.

Now, as he lay there on the couch fully clothed, his boots on the floor next to it, he wished he could have gotten a chance to beat the hell out of Josh for what he'd done to Kelsey.

9

The sun was just coming up when Jimmy heard a noise in Kelsey's kitchen. His first thought was to grab the thick silver candlestick holder off the coffee table in front of him. He was sure Josh had come back, and this time he wasn't going to take any crap from him.

So with the heavy candle stick holder in his hand, he headed for the kitchen, and Josh. However, what he found surprised him. There sat Kelsey at the table; she was holding her face and whimpering with pain.

Jimmy hurried over to her and placed the candle stick holder on the table. He went right to the cabinet where he found the aspirins the night before and pulled out four. He handed her the pills and a glass of water. Then went to the freezer and made her another ice pack. After handing it to her he lifted her up into his arms and carried her to the couch, where he laid her down.

Once he had her settled in, he placed the ice pack on her cheek and eye.

"Kelsey, your face looks pretty bad, and I know for sure your nose is broken. Let me take you to the hospital," he implored.

"No, please don't take me there. There'll be lots of questions, and I'm not up to answering them. Please, Jimmy, I'll be alright here, honestly, I will."

"That, Kelsey, isn't going to happen. You're not staying here alonr so that son of a bitch can come back here and do God knows what to you. No way!" He raised his voice in frustration.

"I have no where to go, I have no family, or even friends!" she argued.

"You have me and the Big 4 family. We're all you need," he insisted.

"I can't impose on you guys."

"Look, when Trent got married, he left us with a free bedroom at the farmhouse. That's where I want you to stay. You'll be safe there since one of us guys are always around. We're either sleeping or eating or just hanging out, so you won't be alone, and Josh doesn't know where we live. At least there you can recuperate, without worrying Josh will come back."

"The guys won't like it," she mumbled.

"Believe me, when the guys hear about this, they're going to be almost as pissed as I am."

"Alright, but if the guys don't approve, I'll come right back here," Kelsey warned.

"Don't worry, they'll approve." He nodded.

That evening, Bobby drove Torrie over to the Big 4 farm house. She was told all about Kelsey's troubles so she came armed with a little black bag in her purse, filled with medicine she thought Kelsey might need.

Torrie walked out of Trent's old room off the kitchen shaking her head when Jimmy asked, "So, what do you think?"

"She sat slowly at the kitchen table with Jimmy and Bobby and took a long ragged breath.

"Yes, her nose is broken. I packed it because she's still bleeding. I'm not positive it's not fractured, but the packing will help it heal straight. Not much I can do about her eye and her swollen face. You did all that could be done, although I did bring her some Motrin 800s. They'll put her to sleep, but if she has a hard time with pain you can give her one," Torrie suggested.

"Where'd you get those pills?" Bobby spoke up.

"I have a doctor friend here in town. I explained her injuries as they were explained to me, and I can see all her problems for myself. My doctor friend knows I'm half way though med school and I understand about these injuries. He also said he would make a house call if necessary," she told them.

Torrie looked over at Jimmy. "This medication will help the pain and the swelling. She also needs lots of sleep because the pain keeps her up half the night. However, she will heal, Jimmy. I'm more worried about what this has done to her inside. I mean up here," she added, pointing to her head. "Kelsey's really down. The girl always makes people smile. She's always struck me as a happy person, even the first time I met her, and this has changed her."

"I'll make sure she's taken care of," Jimmy interrupted her.

"Don't get me wrong, Kelsey's one of our own for sure, but you have been going over and above, so what's really going on here?" Bobby said as he looked Jimmy in the eye.

"Don't worry about it. Just know I'll take care of Kelsey with, or without you guys," Jimmy informed him.

"Damn it, that's not what I meant. I still stand by the fact Kelsey's part of our Big 4 family, period." Bobby raised his voice.

All Jimmy did was nod his agreement.

Once Torrie had explained everything to Jimmy and gave him Doctor Willis's card, her and Bobby headed out the door and over to his truck.

She glanced up at him, and decided he looked awfully serious. It wasn't like him. "What's wrong, Bobby? You aren't mad at Jimmy, are you?"

No, I'm not mad. I just don't understand him. Sure we'll take care of Kelsey. She's one of us for sure. What I don't understand is how possessive he's become with her. Hell, it seems like only a few weeks ago he was head over heals for Tina. Now it's all about Kelsey, Jimmy's really got me confused." He took a deep breath.

"Listen, Bobby, I never said anything before because I was trying to mind my own business."

"You mind your own business?" He chuckled.

"Do you want to hear this, or not?" She glared at him.

"I'm sorry, yes I do want to hear what you have to say." He tried not to laugh.

"Haven't you seen the way Jimmy looks at Kelsey? Hell, Bobby, since the first poker game we played, neither one of them could keep their eyes off of each other. There's been an attraction going on there for a while now."

"I didn't notice." He shrugged.

"It doesn't surprise me." She shook her head at him.

Now Torrie had a thing for Bobby from the first time she met him, but he was clueless about her feelings. Yet it almost seemed as if he wanted his cake and eat it too. He would hold her in his arms, even kiss her, but he would never get too close. Just about the time she thought he really did feel something special for her, he would pull away. One minute he was talking to her like she was his little sister, and the next she would stand there while he brought out the passion in her. *Oh Bobby Weston, you make me crazy.*

A moment later Torrie was tugged from her thoughts. "What do you mean, it doesn't surprise you?" he asked.

"Oh, never mind," she said as she started to walk away.

"No, you don't." He snatched up her hand and pulled her into his arms.

She saw his blue eyes sparkle with devilment. What was he up to?

"Okay, spill it, tell me what you mean." He grinned.

"Alright, I'll tell you. You don't notice anything about me, or the way you treat me for that matter. You're always kissing me, or hugging me, Only to go and treat me like some little kid in the next breath. I'm not a little kid." She raised her voice.

"You know, Torrie, I love it when you're angry."

"Oh, my God, Bobby, you're doing it again. What do you want from me?" she said in a near shout.

At that moment she wanted to kill Bobby Weston, because all he did was was pull her closer, where she experienced a sweet tongue filled, heart pumping kiss which rocked her world. She struggled just a little, until she melted in his arms.

Torrie was still nestled there when he whispered, "Are you ready to go?" The only answer she had the energy for was the nod of her head. Yet when she looked up a satisfying smile filled his face. She thought, now what was that all about?"

Damn it. Torrie thought about his smile, all the way home.

The farmhouse was quiet when Jimmy stepped through Trent's old bedroom door. Kelsey was awake, her head propped up on a pillow. Hell, he couldn't help but feel bad for her. There she lay; a broken woman in body and mind, all because of a brother with a drug problem.

"How are you doing since Torrie took a look at you? Your nose looks better." He tried to sound cheerful.

"How can you say that, Jimmy? My nose is huge, even bigger bandaged up!" she snapped.

He gave her a half smile. "You know, Kelsey, it's alright to be mad, pissed off even at this situation. However, put the blame where it belongs, on your brother. You have to stop letting him get to you. Alright, he beat you, got the best of you, but remember, you don't owe him anything. Not your money, your home and especially not you—Kelsey. Me and the guys are going to do all we can to help you get Josh out of your life. But, you have to fight for what's inside of you, and be the gal we know," Jimmy told her.

"You really believe you can help me, don't you?" She was surprised.

"Hell, yeah I do, and we will, damn it! Still Kelsey, it's up to you if you really want to get rid of the guy who has made your life a living hell."

He saw her give him a half smile.

"I promise you this, Jimmy, if you help me, I'll work just as hard as you do to get my brother out of my life."

He placed a gentle kiss on her forehead. "I'll be here for you, but first we have to get you healed."

Jimmy left the room only to come back almost immediately. With a glass of water in one hand and a Motrin in the other as he said, "We're going to start right now by taking this."

He showed her the large white pill and saw her shake her head at him.

"You're going to take this—now. It's late, and Torrie said this will give you the rest you need."

"You know how I feel about pills."

"I know, but you need it for the pain. I promise I won't give you another pill once you're better," he pledged.

"You promise?"

He traced a cross on his chest. "Cross on my heart."

"Okay, just for you." She popped the pill into her mouth, and swallowed a half a glass of water.

Jimmy knew tonight she would finally get a good night's sleep.

A moment later he sat on the chair next to the bed. His arms were folded across his chest. "Now, rest and heal, I'll be right here," he assured her.

Once he saw she was sound asleep, he sat there staring at her, hoping he could really do everything he promised.

"Damn it, Kelsey," he whispered, "what is it about you that makes me want to keep you from harm, protect you? And I know down deep, I'd even protect you with my life. Why is it I feel this way, you sweet little thing, why?"

The next few days Jimmy stayed with Kelsey, just taking care of her.

Although it was almost a week later when Jimmy stood frying eggs. He turned at a sound of heels on the floor behind him. It was Kelsey. She'd just stepped out of Trent's old bedroom, dressed, and looking through her purse.

"Hey, what's this?" he asked.

"Good morning to you too, Jimmy. I'm going to work today," she announced.

"Oh no, I don't think that's a good idea. Your face is still black and blue."

He watched Kelsey as she sat down at the table and took a piece of toast off a dish in the middle.

"Look, Jimmy, you're right about something. I have to be myself and it starts by putting all this behind me. Josh is not going to take Big 4 away from me. It's not going to happen. I'm also sure the guys need you working on their trucks," she said in between bites.

"Well, to be completely honest, I was going to lock you in and go to work this afternoon. Benet's truck is down," he admitted.

"You see, it's time, Jimmy."

He sat down across the table from her as he set a plate of eggs in front of both of them.

"My only question is, do you really think you're well enough?" he worried out loud.

Jimmy saw Kelsey pour herself a cup of hot water and as she placed a tea bag in the cup he heard her ask, "Want some?"

"No, I have juice and quit changing the subject. Are you well enough?" he repeated.

"I won't lie to you. I'm still as sore as hell, but I swear to you, I need to get out of here, and keep my mind busy."

"It would be good to have you where I can keep an eye on you. That way I won't worry about you when I'm working on the trucks, because all the other guys will be there. Alright, you can go, but with one condition," he conceded.

"Oh, Jimmy, I'm not a kid." She shook her head.

"Listen, this is the condition, take it, or leave it," he growled.

"Alright, what is it?" She took a deep breath.

"If it gets to be too much on you, you let me know?"

"Fine," she said with an attitude.

"Kelsey…?" he warned.

"Oh my God, you're acting like a jealous husband!" She sighed.

All Jimmy did was smile. He guessed he was acting a bit bossy. And you know what? He thought he could live with it.

He sat back watching her eat her eggs, when he realized he was treating her like a wife. Damn, if he could only get the fringe benefits, this could just work out.

All of a sudden he looked up because Kelsey's voice broke the spell. "Why are you staring at me?" she asked suspiciously.

"Can't a man just admire a beautiful woman?"

"Oh yeah, with a big purple eye and swollen face. Oh yeah, I really look like a fashion model." He leaned over the table, took her face gently in his hands and he stole a very sexy kiss.

He hoped his kiss had her thinking of going to bed with him, touching him. Yet, when he pulled away, he just winked at her and said, "Yeah, my kind of fashion model."

He went back to eating his eggs and all she could do was swallow hard.

When they finished, he said, "I'll drive."

"Sounds good," she agreed.

Kelsey was over-whelmed when they walked into the Big 4 office. She was touched with the concern Bobby and Trent showered on her the moment she stepped inside. Their heartfelt thoughts were so genuine, she couldn't help but hug them both.

"Thanks, guys, I owe you all more than I can say. Hey, Trent, how's Candy?" Kelsey asked.

"She's getting bigger every day. You are coming over Christmas day, aren't you?" Trent asked.

"I would love to." Then she kind of stared off into space.

"What's wrong?" Bobby asked.

Kelsey shook it off. "I was just thinking. I'd forgotten Christmas was so close."

"Well, you have been a little preoccupied." Jimmy chuckled.

"I'll have to do some shopping. Oh man, we should have a tree in here," she told them.

"We have some stuff Candy bought last year," Trent said as he placed his hands gently on her shoulders.

"Okay, point me in the right direction and I'll Christmas this place up," Kelsey announced.

It was nearly two in the afternoon when Jimmy's stomach began to talk to him. So he came into the office wiping his hands on a shop rag. It was perfect timing too, because he saw Kelsey unpacking a bag of burgers.

"Hey, where's mine? I'm starving!" Jimmy asked.

He sat on the edge of Bobby's desk, just staring around the office.

"I see you've been busy, Kelsey," Jimmy said, while admiring the twinkling lights.

"Bobby and I did a great job, if I do say so myself. Oh, I'll be right back. I have to put a copy of these contracts on Trent and Benet's desks," she said, then hurried off to her task.

Once she was gone, Jimmy asked, "How's she been, Bobby? Is she okay?"

"Hell, she has more energy than me! She did all this decorating and she's caught up with half her work. However, I am worried about something. What are we going to do about her? Someone can't always be with her. Even if we could, she's a free spirit. We won't be able to keep her down," Bobby said seriously.

"I know. I was going to talk to you about it," Jimmy said quietly.

"Me?" Bobby asked.

"Yes, you have a cop buddy," Jimmy said as he watched for Kelsey.

"Dale?" Bobby's curiosity was peaked.

"Yeah, I want you to talk to him and see what could be done about her brother. Maybe he'll know what our next step should be," Jimmy suggested.

"I'll see if I can see him tonight," Bobby agreed.

"Who are you seeing tonight, Bobby? Got a hot date?" Kelsey asked from across the room.

"No, just thought I'd see an old friend of mine." He winked at Jimmy and they both went back to eating.

Later that night, Jimmy sat waiting for Bobby to come home. It wasn't long before he came in through the back door and into the living room and he watched Bobby turn the lights on.

There was Jimmy sitting in the darkness. He smiled as Bobby took a deep breath and turned on Jimmy. "What the hell are you doing? You scared ten years off my damn life!"

Jimmy chuckled. "Good, you've done it to me a time or two. Remember when Tina and I were kissing on the couch and you popped up between us? I thought my heart was going to jump out of my chest. And what about the time I was working on my truck out back and you threw a smoke bomb underneath it. I didn't know what the hell was going on," Jimmy reminded him.

"That was hysterical. I wished I had a camera, because the look on your face was priceless. I swear you looked like you were gonna pass out." Bobby couldn't stop laughing.

"And what about when you…?"

"Alright, alright, I get it. I guess we're even," Bobby cut him off.

"Hell, no, we're not," Jimmy informed him.

"Alright, Jimmy, you can just chill." Bobby grinned.

Jimmy saw Bobby sit down slowly on the couch where he clasped his hands between his knees and said with seriousness, "I guess you stayed up to hear what Dale said."

"And…?" Jimmy prodded.

"He pretty much told me what I already knew. There has to be a police report because once you have proof she was beaten, she can put a restraining order out on her brother.

However, Dale did say if she was afraid for her life, she could get a different type of restraining order. But remember, she has to name all the places she goes so they could be added to the restraining order," Bobby explained.

"How in the hell does that help? Even with the order Josh could beat Kelsey to death before she could even call the cops." Jimmy shook his head.

"That's exactly what Dale said. The cops have to catch him on her property, or at least one that's been named on the restraining order, before the guy could go to jail. So my friend, we're back to square one." Bobby took a deep breath.

Jimmy stood and paced the floor. "So, she's damned if she does and damned if she doesn't."

"Oh, Dale did say if the police can catch him in the act, or if this happens again, she can file a police report and an assault charge. He could be tried in court for bodily injury. That's the lesser crime of murder. The guy would go away for a very long time."

"She'd have to get the hell beat out of her again. No way!" Jimmy insisted.

"Now, what are you going to do with this information?"

"I don't know, Bobby. I can't watch her every second and even if I could, she sure as hell wouldn't let me. I do know she can't go back home. He knows where she lives. He's probably watching her place right now, just waiting for her to come home. I guess we'll have to at least go after the bodily injury restraining order. That being said, there's something I'll have to talk to you and Benet about," Jimmy said.

"You want her to move in here, don't you?" Bobby asked.

"Well, kind of. I'll take you and Benet out to breakfast once I take Kelsey to work in the morning, so we can talk."

"What about Trent? He'll be there. Tuesday is still the day he does his paperwork," Bobby told him.

"Someone has to be there to keep an eye on Kelsey. I'll explain it all to him later," he said.

"Yeah, he's there like clockwork so he can keep an eye on her, unless Candy has the baby."

"Damn, I forgot all about Candy. How is she, Bobby?"

"She's huge, man, and swollen like a balloon. But as soon as Candy has the baby, Torrie is coming home for two weeks. She's cleared it with her professors." Bobby grinned.

Jimmy smacked Bobby on the back. "You sure as hell won't mind now will you? When are you going to tell Torrie the way you feel about her?"

"When you tell Kelsey the way you feel about her!" Bobby turned the tables.

"I tried. I thought we were really going somewhere. Hell, we talked, shared our feelings, even kissed. And all of a sudden this bullshit with her brother went down. Believe me, this is not the time to strike up a romance." Jimmy shook his head.

"Finally, someone is in my shoes, because right now is not the time to push romance on Torrie, while the girl is trying to be a doctor." Bobby slapped Jimmy on the back.

"I understand, but the electricity between you and Torrie could light up a room."

"Yeah, and I'd sure as hell like to be electrified by her." Bobby chuckled.

A moment later Jimmy saw the devilish look on Bobby's face and couldn't help but laugh right out loud.

10

Jimmy kept his promise to take the guys out to breakfast the very next morning. So, just after the sun came up, he sat at a table with Benet and Bobby at Johnny's home cooking restaurant.

All three men were staring out the wide front window while sipping their morning cup of steaming hot coffee.

Jimmy's attention was drawn to the biggest of the Big 4 truckers. His partner had his chair rocking on two legs near the wall. He was waiting for Benet and his chair to crumble to the floor any moment when the questions began.

"So, what was so all fired important we couldn't discuss this at the office?" Benet asked.

Jimmy looked up at the guys as a whole. "Look, I need to talk to both of you. However, I don't want to discuss this in front of Kelsey."

"So, this is about Kelsey?" Benet said with confidence.

"Just hold your horses, Benet, let me tell you what I found out. I had Bobby talk to his friend Dale," Jimmy said when Benet opened his mouth to speak.

"You mean his cop friend?" Benet asked.

"Yep, seems Kelsey should have filed a police report, which she didn't do. So now she can't get a restraining order, at least not for the beating he just gave her. But I'm determined to get her another type of restraining order.

There is one you can get because she fears for her life. Yet even when she gets one, they have to catch her brother there. And what are the chances Kelsey would be able to call the cops if he comes after her?" Jimmy explained

"Not a hell of a good one." Benet shook his head.

"Exactly, which leaves her between a rock and a hard place." Jimmy nodded.

"I get it, but what can we do about it? Would you like me to kill the guy? Actually, I could make it look like an accident. My Peterbilt rig won't even see him crossing the street when I run his ass over," Benet joked.

"Actually, that's a pretty good idea, Benet. Although, I don't think our business could take losing you to Vehicular Manslaughter charges." Jimmy chuckled.

Jimmy watched Benet lean over the table and speak so only his friends could hear. "I'll swear on a stack of bibles I never saw the guy."

"Look, Benet, I think I have an idea where no one has to get hurt, or go to jail. You know the old flat we have on the third floor? We let Kelsey live there. One of us is always around, so I don't think she'll be afraid there. Moreover, we can make sure she's safe," Jimmy said.

"Hell, that place isn't fit for man, nor beast," Benet said with a shake of his head.

"No one's ever lived up there. How can we put her up there? And why can't she just stay where she is, in Trent's old room?" Bobby asked.

"Because a woman needs privacy, especially living with three men. C'mon, guys, you know we're a pain in the ass. And it won't be long before she's pushing to go back to her flat, or worse, run from her brother," Jimmy insisted.

"Look, if you can get Kelsey to stay there, I'll help you fix the place up." Benet sat back and inhaled the aroma of his hot breakfast the waitress placed in front of him.

"You can count on me, too. But what if she insists on going back to her flat?" Bobby said as he slathered jelly on his toast.

"Don't worry, let me handle Kelsey," Jimmy said as he cut the ham on his plate.

"Have you spoken with Trent? You know he still owns a quarter of the farm house. We shouldn't really make any decisions without talking to him, too," Benet said.

"Trent likes Kelsey as much as we do. I don't think he'll mind one bit, but I will ask him," Jimmy told them.

So with a nod from his partners, they all dug into their breakfast.

That very same evening Jimmy and his two partners sat in the living room as he shouted for Kelsey. A few moments later he saw her enter the room in sweat pants and an over-sized T shirt.

"What's up guys?" she asked with a wide smile.

Jimmy saw Benet and Bobby look over at him, just as the front door opened and Trent walked in.

Jimmy watched as Trent sat in the recliner in the corner and gave everyone a big smile.

The room went quiet while Jimmy worried if Kelsey would take what they were about to offer. He needed her to be close and safe. Or, was it really because of the way he dreamt of her, his constant need to kiss and touch her? That thought gave him the lump in his throat?

Jimmy had to admit, it was about the way he felt, but it was also about keeping her safe. Then he noticed Kelsey gave all the guys a serious look.

"How's Candy, Trent?" Kelsey asked. "Today you said she had a doctor's appointment."

"The doc said any day now. I think she couldn't be any happier to have the baby. Poor thing feels like hell. However, that's not what we're here to talk about." Trent grinned.

"Is there a problem with my work?" Kelsey worried out loud.

"No honey, your work is great. We couldn't be any happier with what you're doing at Big 4," Benet answered.

"Hell, in two days you have nearly caught up on most of your work, and you were off for over a week," Bobby interrupted.

"So what's the problem?" she asked again.

It was Jimmy who answered her. "The four of us have decided you can't go back to your flat."

He didn't like the tears he saw welling up in her eyes as she slowly sat on the couch between Benet and Bobby.

"You're right. I'm sure Josh is waiting for me to come back to my place so he can get what he came for. I think maybe it's time for me to go. I will leave whatever I have at the flat, just take my sewing machine and what money I have in the bank. I'll have to start fresh again in some other state," she said with sadness in her voice.

Jimmy squatted down in front of her, took both her hands in his and looked into her tearful eyes.

"Kelsey, if you run now, you'll be running from Josh your whole life. At some point you're going to have to make a stand."

"If I stand for myself he'll come after me, maybe even kill me this time. Isn't my life worth something?" ahe cried.

Jimmy and his partners sat quietly, just watching the emotion flow out of Kelsey. This was a side of her the guys at Big 4 had never seen before. Even Jimmy only saw a bit of her vulnerability when she was in pain from her beating.

So Jimmy went on, "Kelsey your life is worth everything to us. We said you are part of the Big 4 family and we meant it. We have an idea, one we think will help you make a stand of sorts, with people who care about you. People who will take care of you, even protect you if need be."

It broke his heart as he watched her wipe the tears from her eyes with her hand. He was sure they burned because they were now red.

"I don't understand. How can you do all of that? You can't be with me twenty four, seven," Kelsey said as she wiped her eyes again.

"We want you to stay here, Kelsey, where you can stand for yourself. Where you'll be safe," Bobby spoke up.

"I can't stay here forever. You guys have your own lives to live," she blubbered.

Jimmy had hold of her hand when he pulled her off the couch and led her up the stairs. The rest of the guys followed right behind them. They went up two flights of stairs to a dirty, spider-webbed, old fashioned door with a dusty crystal door knob.

Jimmy gave it a push with his shoulder and the door flew open.

He helped her up three more steps and Kelsey stood there, staring.

The stairs were all encased in spider webs. Yet moments later, he had led her into the middle of the dirtiest little flat in town.

The living room was large. Three single, old looking, white, wood windows looked as though they would flood the front of the farm house with lots of bright light in the daytime.

To the left of the living room was an old door Jimmy observed as she walked over and opened it to a bedroom. The closet was deep and all under the eaves. The room also had an old fashioned wooden slide window.

Then he watched her intently as she walked back through the living room to an open forties style kitchen. Again the kitchen looked old. A white porcelain deep farm sink was surrounded by ceramic tiles which lined the counters. They looked every bit of dusty brown as the rest of the place.

Jimmy held his breath as she looked out the back door at nearly three flights of stairs to the bottom.

He wanted her to like it because he was convinced this would solve her problem.

So he waited anxiously as she turned to the truckers. Jimmy couldn't wait to hear what she thought of the place.

"What do you think? We know it needs work, and we'll be happy to fix anything needing repair. We're all pretty handy, although, I think Jimmy is the best," Trent told her.

"Guys, I really appreciate this. It's a great flat, but I can't move in. I would be taking advantage of the situation. You guys are just too good to me." She sniffled.

"Look, every one of us wants to be sure you're safe and we think this is the best way to do it. So, you see, we kill two birds with one stone." Benet, the quiet one, stepped into the conversation.

"Benet's right. You'll have your freedom back, we're out of your hair, and you get a flat out of it too," Bobby told her.

"I just can't live here for free, it's not right…" She wiped her eyes again.

Jimmy stopped her in the middle of her sentence. "This is an empty flat. Better someone lives here, than it stays empty and goes to hell." He leaned close to her. "One of us is always around if you should need us. Believe me, Josh won't come here."

"What about my things?" she worried out loud.

"We'll have a moving company deliver it all to Big 4 Trucking. You take what you want as you need it. Jimmy can carry it in his capped pick up because I'm sure your brother will be watching to find out where you are," Trent explained.

"Yeah, great idea, Trent. I'll make sure her stuff gets up here to her," Benet said.

"And I'll make sure she always rides to work with one of us," Bobby added.

"Yeah, Bobby, we could figure out a schedule for each week." Trent had that good idea.

"I'll make arrangements for the movers. I know some pretty good guys," Bobby said.

"That's all well and good guys, but what about the rent?" Kelsey asked.

Jimmy spoke calmly. "By you living here, you save us worry and you also keep the place in good shape. Once all of this is behind us, we can reevaluate, but for now, let's just call it a perk of your job."

"Well, I guess you guys have it all figured out. So this must be my new flat," Kelsey said with a deep breath.

One by one the guys gave her a hug and headed down the stairs. All but Jimmy. He stood leaning against the kitchen sink smiling.

"What?" Kelsey looked suspicious.

"You made a real good decision, Kelsey." Jimmy nodded.

He saw her lean against the half wall which divided the kitchen from the living room.

"You guys really took time to figure this all out, didn't you?"

He shrugged. "It was just the right thing to do."

"You found out, didn't you?" she asked.

"Found out what?"

"There isn't much I can do about Josh. Chances are he could kill me one day."

Jimmy stared down at the dirty kitchen floor. "He's not going to kill you. I won't let him and neither will the guys." He walked across the kitchen to her and she lifted his face with both hands so he'd look into her eye.

"The last time Josh beat me he nearly killed me. I had enough of the abuse and of being afraid all the time. I only worked to exist. So I went to the police, sat down with the precinct Sergeant. He told me all about the system and what they could do for me. And it seemed to me, no matter how I did it, there was still a chance for Josh to beat me, kill me, if he wanted. Because like you and the guys, the cops can't be there every minute. Although I do have to admit they got me out of the city and set me up in my first town. That seemed to be my only way out. So, here I am nearly six years later, faced with the same damn problem. I thought I was pretty good at covering my trail. Guess I wasn't." She shrugged.

He stood there as Kelsey searched his eyes for any clue of what he was thinking. His sparkling eyes gave her none.

It wasn't what she said, as it was the way she looked in her sweats and short spiked hair which made him take a deep breath at the sight of those tiny, delicate earrings which hung from her kissable looking ear lobes. Because now all he could think about was ravaging her. Yet the look in her eyes brought him back to the conversation.

"Yes, I know all about restraining orders, but you have to understand, you didn't have us six years ago," Jimmy told her.

He placed his hands on hers. "We'll take this one day at a time. We start Saturday morning." Without another word, he took her hand and led her back down the stairs.

The following Saturday, Jimmy and the other guys woke to the sound of a brush scrubbing a floor.

It was Jimmy who entered the 3rd floor flat first. He was sipping a steaming hot cup of coffee, holding another cup in his other hand for Kelsey. She leaned back on her heels from her scrubbing and took the warm cup of coffee he handed her.

"Thanks, this smells wonderful." She beamed up at him.

Jimmy leaned against the kitchen wall and saw a shiny clean kitchen. The 1940's style wide stove sparkled and the refrigerator was nearly as shiny as it was back in the 40's. He motioned his head to the old appliances. "Do you think they work?"

"The refrigerator does. I think the pilot light just has to be lit on the stove," she told him.

Jimmy pulled a lighter out of his pocket and showed it to her, "This will tell the tale." He grinned.

"You don't smoke, do you?" She was taken back.

"No, but you'd be surprised how many times I use this thing." He lit the pilot on the stove and turned on a burner and announced, "Perfect."

"You really are Mr. Fix it," she said as she watched the burner glow.

Jimmy gave her a hand up off the floor and asked, "What else do you need done?"

He smiled at the view of her sway while she walked over to a closet where she opened a short door and pointed inside.

Jimmy gave her a strange look and peered in. It was a deep storage area where an old sofa, chair, even end tables had been stored. He looked back out at her.

"I could use the furniture," she said.

"They're filthy." He was appalled.

"I can clean them, you'll see, they'll look great."

"What's filthy?" Bobby and Benet asked in unison when they walked in.

"Look at this," Jimmy said.

He led his partners over to the storage wall and all three gaped inside.

Kelsey wanted to laugh at the three backsides sticking out of the hole in the wall. Yet she kept her composure.

When they all turned to her, the smile on her face was contagious, although she continued to hold back her laughter at the sight of their three wide grins.

"Are you sure you want all this stuff?" Benet asked. "It's pretty dirty."

"You'd be surprised what a little elbow grease can do," she assured them.

"If you're sure, we'll get the furniture out of there for you." Bobby assured her.

A moment later, Kelsey stood there shaking her head as the men argued about who would get in the storage wall first. She found they made the decision just like they made all the decisions at work, by shouting at each other. And from experience, she also knew whose voice was loudest, won.

Suddenly there was a loud shout and she understood Benet won the honor of squeezing into the hole in the wall first. Bobby went in right after him.

Once the two truckers were in the tiny space, all Kelsey could hear was their muffled voices. She couldn't understand everything, but she knew they were swearing at one another.

"Damn it, Bobby, lift your end, quit being such a wuss!"

"Who are you calling a wuss, Benet? I'm not complaining about the dusty, cramped quarters, so shut your damn mouth before I put my fist in it!" Bobby yelled.

"Why don't you try it, Bobby, go on!" Benet roared.

"Guys, you're supposed to be getting the furniture out, not finding a small area for the two of you to punch yourselves silly, now get that stuff out of there!" Jimmy shouted into the hole in the wall.

"Now, why'd ya go and piss Jimmy off?" Benet said as he stared at Bobby.

"Me...? Oh, shut up Benet, and let's move this damn furniture!" Bobby said in frustration.

Kelsey was vacuuming the furniture when she noticed Jimmy and Bobby were washing the living room walls while Benet did the bedroom walls. She shut off the vacuum and watched these ever so sweet men. They were going out of their way to help her. She'd never seen such great guys in her life. Her father wasn't a good father and definitely not a good human being either. It seemed like Josh was made from the same cloth. Here these men, strangers really, were helping her, not only with the work around the flat, but watching out for her too.

"What's wrong?" Jimmy spoke and she lost her thoughts.

"Nothing," she shrugged.

"That look on your face said something is."

"I was just thinking about the men in my life, until now that is." She stared off.

As Kelsey and Jimmy talked, Benet heard only part of the conversation. He wanted to hear more so he came and leaned against the door frame and listened which caught Bobby's attention, so he did the same.

"What do you mean until now?" Jimmy asked.

She took a deep breath, then said, "The men in my life have been mostly family and they definitely had their problems. However, you guys, well hell, you treat me better than they ever did. I don't deserve you guys." She looked down at the floor.

A moment later she smiled when Jimmy took her into his arms and hugged her. "You do deserve to be treated well. You're a woman for God sakes. You don't owe your brother anything, not one blessed thing."

She became choked up and Jimmy acted as though he didn't notice.

"Now forget about your family. You have us and we'll be here for you, so get back to work," he said as he gave her a little squeeze.

She couldn't help but smile at the grin he was giving her and she turned the vacuum back on and continued cleaning the furniture.

A few hours later, Kelsey shook her head at Benet, Bobby and Jimmy while they struggled with a bed. They were having a heck of a time getting it up those last three steps of the staircase.

Kelsey had never heard such cursing. She had to lean over the newly polished railing and shout, "What the hell are you guys doing?"

"Trying to get this son of a bitchin' bed up these frigin stairs!" Benet snapped.

"Where'd you get the bed?" she asked.

"Trent's old room," Jimmy grinned up at her.

"You can't do that. What if he wants it?" she argued.

A moment later she stepped back because they finally made the turn with the box springs into the sparkling clean flat.

"I talked to Trent. He's cool with it." Bobby answered her question.

"Yeah, and he's not leaving his little eye Candy anytime soon," Benet added.

"Eye Candy?" She didn't look as though she understood.

"Yeah, it's the big joke. He used to call her Eye Candy, but if you said it, he'd take your head off," Jimmy explained.

"Yeah, he was extremely touchy about it. He wanted everyone to call her Candice, which only made us want to call her Eye Candy all the more," Benet said with a chuckle as he got caught between the door and the box springs.

"Yep, that really pissed him off." Bobby took up the telling when he gave the box springs a shove.

"I swear he wanted to kill us nearly every time we saw her. All kidding aside, though, there's no better girl for Trent than Candy. Those two went through hell just to be together. And to be honest with you, there isn't one of us who wouldn't go through fire for either one of them." Jimmy said.

Suddenly Kelsey and Bobby couldn't stop laughing because Bobby gave the box springs another push and both Jimmy and Benet hit the floor.

It was late Saturday night when Kelsey finally sat alone on the freshly cleaned couch with Jimmy.

"I want to thank you again for everything, Jimmy." She beamed up at him.

"If you want to thank me, come over here and give me a kiss," he teased.

"Oh, my boss and landlord would like a favor," she joked.

"No Kelsey, I told you I'm not your boss anymore and the guys and I are not charging you rent. It's just me, Jimmy, who wants a kiss."

Kelsey slid across the couch and made herself comfortable in his lap.

"I could definitely be talked into kissing you Jimmy." She seemed shy.

"I don't want to talk—I want a kiss." He stopped in front of her.

Kelsey didn't get a chance to say another word because Jimmy's mouth claimed hers. She loved his hot, searing lips when they captured her and made her feel unbelievably sexy.

It seemed to her neither one of them could get enough. His lips tasted hers over and over again. Her whole body seemed to surrender to him. Kelsey knew by the way he held her, he wanted it all from her and for the moment she was ready to give it.

Her head leaned back into his arms and he ravaged her throat and earlobes. It seemed as though he was making love to her ears with his tongue, The fire he was stoking had her body aching for his touch and wanting more.

Heat surged through her when his hand moved slowly up her body under her oversized T shirt and when he unclasped her bra, Kelsey stopped breathing.

She started to tremble as his fingers slid around and touched her breast. And a moment later she thought she'd swallow her tongue when his fingers encircled her nipples.

Heaven help her. She knew he had her in his control and she couldn't seem to get enough. Oh hell, she didn't want to stop him either. Then his husky voice rang in her ear, it brought chills to her whole body. "Shall we take this to your bed?" he whispered.

Somehow his deep voice brought her back from the depths of her passion. And she pulled out of his grasp.

"Jimmy, I'm not sure about this. I need a shower and this is my first night here…" She sounded like she'd run a mile.

"Damn it, Kelsey, why did you let me go so far?" he snapped.

She stared at him as if he were crazy, "Remember, Jimmy, I didn't start this."

"You're right. I started it, but damn it all, you know how I feel about you." He heaved a sigh.

"I care about you too. It isn't easy for me to say no either, but I want to take this slow, Jimmy. I don't want to be a one night stand. And I definitely don't want the only thing we have in common to be sex!"

"That's not true, we talk, and laugh, you and I, It's not all about sex. Still, you have to admit there are definitely sparks between us."

She sat back down on the couch next to him and rubbed her open palms on her upper thighs. "Yeah, I don't think you and I are going to have any trouble in that department." She grinned.

Kelsey's sweet statement calmed Jimmy right down and all he could do was laugh. It wasn't long before Kelsey was laughing too.

"Okay, if you don't want to make love to me…"

"Now, I didn't say I didn't want to make love to you. I just want to take it slow," she cut him off.

"Alright little Miss lets take it slow, what are we gona do now?" he asked.

She hurried into the kitchen, reached in the drawer and pulled out a deck of cards, paper and pencil.

"What's this?" Jimmy sounded suspicious.

"We can play poker."

"Oh no, you're not practicing your card skills on me, girl. I still remember when you took all my money when we played at Trent's house a few months back. I barely got out of there with my shirt."

"Okay, how about Gin, penny a point?" She giggled.

"You're on!"

11

It was late at night when there was an urgent knock on Tina's door. She hurried to answer it hoping it was Jimmy, Wishing he'd changed his mind about her, realized he loved her, or at least wanted the pleasure she could give him. Either way, she would take it and him back. So she opened the door with the biggest smile.

However, in that instant her beautiful expression turned to disappointment.

"Josh, what the hell are you doing here? I thought we had a deal."

"We did, but the stakes have changed."

"What do you mean, changed?" She looked worried.

"Seems my sister has a guardian looking after her," he said as he walked past her into the apartment.

She slammed the door and glared at him. "Start making sense. What the hell are you talking about?"

He plopped down into a wide barrel chair in the corner of the dining room and gave her the same glare back. "Your buddy; your boyfriend, isn't his name, Jimmy?" Josh smirked.

"Yeah, and what did he do?" she asked.

"He came to my sister's aid, broke my nose, gave me a black eye and knocked me unconscious," Josh informed her.

She watched him lean forward out of the shadows where she could see the slight discoloration of the bruises on his face. "All this means nothing to me. You told me she'd run after you talked to her," she said. "She was so afraid of you she'd head out of town, her tail between her legs. Now you're whining. I paid you to do a job and you sure as hell haven't kept your end of the deal."

"Look, I can't scare my sister out of town if she constantly has someone guarding her. If it isn't your boyfriend, it's one of his buddies," Josh blurted out.

"Buddies…?" She questioned.

"Yeah, those guys he works with. They're all helping her. Your boyfriend even moved her in with him!"

"Into the farmhouse…?" She couldn't believe it.

"Yes, it looks like a farmhouse. I watched him take her there the day after he nearly killed me. She ain't been alone since. He, or his buddies, had all her stuff taken from her flat and put into storage."

Tina slowly sat on the chair across from him and stared off into space. "He moved her in with him?" she said in almost a whisper.

Suddenly she had a flash-back. She and Jimmy were lying in bed when she asked him to move in with her. She remembered all he did was chuckle. He said it would ruin their relationship and now he'd moved Kelsey into the farmhouse, his home.

A moment later she couldn't even swallow the heart breaking lump in her throat.

All of a sudden Josh's voice snapped her back into reality and the conversation they were having.

"That's how it looks. He moved her in, and I'll tell you something else, Kelsey's never alone. Someone takes her to work, someone takes her shopping and some one takes her home. They watch her like a hawk."

"So what are you telling me, Josh? Are you saying you can't keep your end of the bargain?" She squinted at him.

"No Tina, I just can't get to her right now. I'm just gonna need time for your boyfriend and his buddies to let their guard down. In the meanwhile, I'm gonna need more money."

"Look Josh, I'm not an endless pit of money here. You have almost all my life's savings now!"

"I'm telling you if you want your boyfriend back, I need five thousand dollars more." She stood up again and stared at him.

"If I give you five thousand more, that's the end of it. I'm cleaned out, and damn it, I haven't seen you produce any results!" she said in a near shout.

"Give me the five grand and I promise I can take care of the rest. You'll have your boyfriend back and I'll have my sister working for me again," he boasted.

"I don't give a damn what's between brother and sister. I just want her out of Jimmy's life!" She slammed her fist on the table.

Tina went to her desk in the corner where she sat and wrote Josh a check and handed it to him. "Now this is it, Josh."

"I told you we had a deal and we do." He pulled the check out of her hand.

"Alright, I expect to see some sort of progress," she demanded.

"Look, you found me and begged me to help you. So you'll have to trust me, trust I can get the job done. And by the way, how did you find me?"

"I know a computer guy who's good at finding people and who they know. So we did a thorough search on Kelsey." She shrugged.

"Isn't that illegal?"

"Lots of things are, but if no one gets hurt, who cares. All I want is for you to get her out of town. I get Jimmy back and no one gets hurt," she said as a matter of fact.

Josh stood up and glared down at her. "I can't promise Kelsey won't get hurt, cause she owes me years worth of money. And I'll be damned if she's not going to pay me."

"Look, Josh, all I want is for her to get out of town. I hired you to get rid of her," she reminded him.

"Don't blow a gasket. Kelsey and I are just going to have a little talk."

"And I get Jimmy back."

Tina watched Josh hurry out the door deep in thought. She assumed he was trying to figure out what he was going to do. She stared at the door long after he left.

Worry ruffled her brow because she was concerned about what he might do. Although, she told him she didn't want Kelsey hurt. The truth was, at this point, she didn't care what happened to her. She just wanted her man back.

A second later her thoughts went back to Josh. There was no doubt about it, he was certainly a loose cannon. Maybe she shouldn't have given him the money, made him wait until the job was finished. No, he wouldn't have gone for that. He had money on his mind when he walked in the door. And what was the strange look in his eyes? He sure was an odd one.

She couldn't help but put it and him out of her mind. No, she couldn't think of him right now. He was only a way to a means, her way of getting Jimmy back. Soon this would be all over and she'd have Jimmy back in her arms again, right where he belonged.

Josh wasn't in the car long when he drove into a secluded driveway just outside of town, where a dark stranger slid into the passenger seat.

"Did you get the money?" the stranger asked.

"Yeah." Josh waved the check in the man's face.

"Five thousand bucks. I told you she'd give it to me. All the damn woman can think about is her precious Jimmy."

"How long do you think you can string her along, and get more money out of her?" the stranger snapped.

"We either do the job or get out of town. I think we've gotten all we're gonna get out of this pigeon," Josh said as he watched nervously in the rearview mirror.

"So brother, are we out of here?" the stranger blurted out.

"No, your sister's going to pay, and big time!" Josh informed him.

"Look, Josh, we got the money. Just let it go," the man hissed.

"Listen, Billy, she owes me," Josh said as he grabbed the guy's collar. "She just up and left me to rot in Detroit!"

Josh cringed when Billy pushed him away. Josh's blood ran cold when Billy's switch blade snapped open. Seconds later his knife was at Josh's throat.

"Don't touch me again, Josh, this is your last warning. I'll gut you like a pig if you go after Kelsey," Billy announced. "I want no part of it, she's my sister—your sistser, too. We have money. I want my share and I'm out of here. If you come, fine, if not, you're on your own."

"What kind of damn brother are you? You desert me when I need you the most," Josh said in disbelief.

He watched Billy like a hawk until he lowered the knife and sat comfortably back into the seat.

"Look Josh, I'm a son of a bitch. I'd slit your throat as soon as look at ya, but I'm not sick enough to beat the hell out of our own sister, maybe even kill her. No, I draw the line right there," Billy insisted.

"So, you don't care that she left me high and dry in downtown Detroit?" Josh raised his voice.

Josh's eyes grew wide as Billy leaned close to his brother. "You're blaming her for finally getting wise to you? She should have done it long before. You nearly killed her twice. And I'll tell you what, if she hadn't left, I would have killed you myself for what you did to her. You're lucky I didn't know what you were doing at the time. So don't look for sympathy from me."

"So why in the hell did you come with me?"

"I came because I thought it was a pretty good scam. Take some money from a crazy lady and leave. It's nice and safe, Josh, but damn, you always have to go too far. Messing up Kelsey's life like you did wasn't in the deal," Billy told him.

"You're not gonna help me are you?" Josh shook his head.

"Tomorrow morning we cash this check at the bank and I'm out of here. I'm only in it for the money. Don't ever forget that!" Billy warned.

Josh wanted to punch Billy when he got out of the car and leaned inside, saying, "I'll be ready at 10 am. Be here, don't make me go looking for ya." And he slammed the door shut.

He sat back in his seat as his brother got into his own car. Josh wasn't afraid of anyone. Anyone that is, but Billy. His brother was good with that knife of his. He'd seen him use it many times. Swore he'd never get on the other end of Billy's anger.

At first Josh thought of getting out of town with the money and keeping it all for himself. Suddenly he rubbed his throat as he thought of his brother's knife there. No, he'd keep the bargain. It was safer, especially when it came to Billy.

He knew once Billy was out of his way he would go after Kelsey. Sooner or later, those guys would leave her alone and he'd make his move. He was ready to take her money and teach her a lesson. She'd learn to do as he told her or she would be very sorry.

12

It had been nearly a month since Kelsey's altercation with Josh. She'd tried to put it out of her mind and focus on her new flat. Truth was, she was proud of her lovely little place.

Kelsey felt safe because either Bobby or Benet took her to work each day and Jimmy was usually in charge of taking her shopping and home. None of them ever took their eyes off her in public. Even Trent found himself in charge of watching her at work.

She realized Big 4 trucking was totally involved in her life. It seemed to her, even though they were confident everything was under control, there was still worry in their eyes. She guessed it was because of the constant concern her brother could get to her.

So, it really shouldn't have surprised her when the guys came up the stairs of the old farmhouse to see her.

A knock got her full attention, so she hurried over to the door leading downstairs and shouted, "Who is it?"

"Big 4," which was a code word meaning it was one of the guys from Big 4 Trucking.

She opened the door with a big smile and stood back as all four of her bosses filed past her and into the flat.

"What's up guys? Why the long faces?" she asked.

"We have tried extremely hard to cover all the bases with you, Kelsey, yet we still worry. We want to keep you healthy and safe." Trent started off the conversation.

"I know. You guys do so much for me. I could never thank you enough for everything."

"We've decided it's not enough," Jimmy chimed in.

"What are you talking about?" She was a little confused.

"We're talking about right here," Bobby answered her question.

"Yeah, like the back door," Benet announced.

"You're right. But you guys have it bolted and barred," Kelsey admitted.

"We do, but like in any other house, if someone wants in, they'll get in," Benet informed her.

"Are you trying to scare me?" She looked a little worried.

"Of course not, Kelsey," Jimmy tried to assure her.

"There's nothing to worry about and we want to keep it that way." Trent tried to calm her.

"What do you mean, Trent?" she asked.

Kelsey couldn't finish her conversation, when her eyes went wide because Benet raised a truck tire iron and showed it to her.

"What am I supposed to do with that?" Kelsey was taken back.

"It goes next to your bed, just under it. C'mon, I'll show you."

She followed Benet to the bedroom, as did the others.

Kelsey stood there while Benet lay on her bed where he reached down just under it.

"C'mon Bobby, lean over me like your trying to hurt me," Benet told him.

She watched Bobby do just that and Benet pulled the tire iron out and pretended to bash his skull in.

"Ya see, Kelsey, if anyone tries to sneak up on you while you're sleeping, you hit the guy as hard as you can, then run through the door and down the stairs to one of us," Benet explained.

She saw where he put the tire iron. "I'll remember."

"See that you do. It's important," Benet reminded her.

A moment later her attention was drawn to Bobby when he reached under his leather jacket and pulled out a large fancy glass bottle of body oil.

"Why thank you Bobby, how thoughtful," she said.

She couldn't believe he shook his head at her.

"It is a gift, but much more thoughtful than you think," Bobby told her.

She stared at him strangely and he went on. "Look, not only is it a beautiful smelling bottle of body oil, but a weapon as well. Here, take a look."

Kelsey held out her hand and he handed it to her. She couldn't believe how heavy it was.

"You see what I mean, don't you? You leave it here on your dresser. It just looks like a feminine bottle of oil. Only you know about its weight," Bobbie said.

She was feeling the weight of the bottle as the guys watched the light go on in her head. She looked up at them and said, "you're making me safe, even when you guys can't be with me." Kelsey smiled at their humble nods.

A large smile filled her face when Jimmy stepped up and pulled her out of the bedroom, laid her on the living room couch where he handed her a truck sized bright silver wrench.

Kelsey stared at it for a good long while until she looked up at Jimmy with a smile. "How kind of you."

It was just the way she said it that had the guys chuckling.

Until Jimmy took hold of her shoulders.

"Hit him on the head," Benet encouraged.

"I can't reach his head." She sounded a little panicked.

Kelsey laid there while the guys studied the situation and they realized she was right. Her arms were too short. She couldn't reach to hit an intruder in the head.

She noticed Jimmy sat on the couch next to her and all four of them gave the wrench some thought until Bobby said, "Don't worry about hitting him in the head, just keep hitting him. You'll hurt him with that big ass thing and you can get away."

"Believe me, the wrench is heavy enough to slow anyone down," Jimmy said with a nod.

"That's all well and good, but where do I put the thing? On the coffee table?" she asked.

"You see, if you're on the couch fighting for your life, you have help at your fingertips," Jimmy said as he slid the wrench in the back of the couch cushion.

She nodded with understanding. "Thanks."

A moment later Kelsey was pulled off the couch by Jimmy where she saw

Trent reach into the back of his jeans and he slid out a thick, wooden baseball bat and showed it to her.

"This, my dear Kelsey, is called a Louisville Slugger. This is old school and there isn't anything better for protecting yourself."

She watched him turn away from everyone and he gave it a hard swing.

"If you get hit in the stomach, ya automatically puke. If ya get hit in the arm you can bet it's broken and if you get hit in the head you're out for the count. That's a Louisville Slugger!" Trent told her.

Kelsey took the bat into her hands and when she gave it a swing all the guys ducked. After she swung it a second time, Trent placed his hand on the bat to still her next swing.

"Treat it with respect. This is old school at its best." Trent eased it gently out of her hands and placed it next to the refrigerator and the back door.

She smiled when he turned to her. "Whomever comes through the door who isn't invited, you hit it out of the ballpark girl."

Kelsey nodded in agreement and turned to the rest of the guys. "I don't know what to say. I've never had anyone treat me so good, care so much about me. I was blessed when I got hired at Big 4. I won't forget what each one of you brought me nor will I forget what to do with them. I will go over each one of them before I go to sleep at night until I know what and how to do it in my sleep." At that she gave each guy a huge hug.

"How is she ,Trent? No baby yet?" Kelsey asked with concern.

"No, and she's as big as a house. The doctor says it could be tomorrow or two weeks from now. He says babies come when they're ready so she stays miserable and we wait."

"Give her my love, and thanks again, guys."

It wasn't long before her bosses were gone, all except for Jimmy who sat at her kitchen table. She looked at him strangely.

"Are you hungry? I can fix you something if you'd like?"

She wondered what was going on when he looked her right in the eye.

"No, I'm not hungry. It's just that I've been thinking. I'd like to take you to a nice place for dinner. Somewhere we can talk in soft candlelight and enjoy a glass of wine. A nice place where I can hold you in my arms on the dance floor and whisper sweet words in your ear.

She sat slowly down across from him. "I don't have any clothes here for the kind of place you're talking about."

Kelsey watched his smile leave his face. "But my clothes are in the back room at Big 4. I'll look for something. Can we do it tomorrow night?"

"You're on, Kelsey. I'll make the reservations." He now wore a grin when he stood to leave.

"Tomorrow, Kelsey. Just you and me," he said with confidence.

"I'll be ready."

Six thirty p.m the next evening, Kelsey was putting the finishing touches on her make up when she heard a knock at her door. She stuck her head out of the bedroom and shouted, "Who is it?"

"Big 4, it's your date."

Again she shouted, "Come in." As Jimmy walked in she yelled again, "I'll be right out."

When she walked out he stood in front of the coffee table in a dark blue, double breasted suit. A white shirt and a dark blue tie beneath it. His hands were clasped together in front of him. God, he looked good.

Then she noticed a beautiful vase full of red roses sitting on the coffee table. There must have been over two dozen flowers in the vase, surrounded by white baby's breath. So, with excitement in her voice, she asked, "Are those for me?"

"Yep, hope you like red." She leaned over and gave a rose a sniff, "I love roses, especially red, but I've never had one given to me."

"Well, you have now."

Kelsey smiled as Jimmy looked her body up and down. She was hoping he thought she looked good in her short, little black dress. A tiny necklace of red beads graced her neck. The same type of beads hung gently from her ears.

Suddenly she realized the only thing left of the little Goth girl was the short frosted spiked hair. She prayed he thought the whole look fit her just right.

Kelsey wondered why his hands were still stacked on top of one another. He sure looked stiff and nervous. She wanted him to relax so she stepped in front of him and slid her fingers over his lapels. "You look handsome, Jimmy."

She sighed as his fingers slid over her curves in her short little black dress.

"Damn, if you don't look good enough to eat!"

"Is that good or bad?" she said breathlessly.

Almost instantly her lips tingled with the luscious kiss he gave her. Her eyes were still closed when he said, "That Kelsey, is very good. However, we better go now before I rip your dress right off you." He looked at her as if he'd do exactly what he said.

So a moment later she shook off the effects of his kiss and hurried to the door. She did it so quickly Jimmy couldn't help but laugh out loud.

Kelsey pulled her coat out of the closet by the door and started to put it on when Jimmy hollered, "Don't you dare. It's my job to help you with your coat."

She was surprised when he took it out of her hands and held it out for her. Kelsey didn't argue, just slid into it. She beamed up at him when he held out his elbow and her arm slid through it and down the stairs they went.

Once down in the driveway she was led to the passenger side of his truck where he opened the door for her and she stepped inside. She smiled while he made sure she was all tucked into the truck and closed the door behind her.

Kelsey sat quietly. She was thinking how wonderful this all was. The flowers, the help with her coat, he even opened the truck door for her, heaven help her. She felt just like a queen.

Now she was excited about what was coming next. So she looked over at him and asked, "Where are we going?"

"That, Kelsey, is a surprise."

"Give me a hint," she prodded.

"A hint, huh?" He gave her question some thought.

"Yeah, you know, like some sort of clue."

"I know what a hint is, Kelsey. I'm just trying to think of a good one. Okay, it's very, very romantic, oh, and it's on the water." He grinned and she thought he looked devilish.

"That's too many hints," she told him. He just shook his head at her silliness.

A short while later they pulled into a restaurant parking lot where the sign read, Breakers on the Bay.

"I know this place," Kelsey said with excitement. "I've never been here, but I've heard it's very expensive."

"We're not counting pennies tonight. Remember, tonight is all about you and me."

She nodded and he led her into the restaurant.

They had a table in a private corner which over-looked the bay in the moonlight. She slid her fingers over the white starched table cloth and placed her crisp green napkin in her lap.

"Do you like sweet wine, or dry?" he asked.

"Sweet, please."

They talked and shared stuffed mushrooms when Jimmy insisted she try the lobster, which she found was wonderful.

They sipped their second glass of wine as they shared a slice of strawberry covered cheesecake which had him smiling at the way she licked her lips.

A moment later Kelsey decided to ask him something she'd been wondering about. "Now Jimmy, you know all about my past, and I know nothing about yours except for the fact your parents drank and you ended up in an orphanage

"Not much to tell, Kelsey. I wasn't big with the girls or even the guys for that matter. I was considered an ignorant grease monkey." He shrugged. "My young life wasn't much fun. I tried to stay away from my parents when they were drinking. If I didn't, it would only warrant a beating. Until one night they were killed in a car accident. They were drinking, of course. And before I knew it, I ended up in a home for boys. Thank God my favorite thing to do was making motors run. It kept me sane," he said as he swirled the wine around in his glass.

She smiled when he grinned over at her. "How great is it to get something that doesn't work to work? I love giving power to a car, a truck, even a lawn mower. It's always fascinated me and still does to this day. I love figuring out the problem and get it back on the road again."

"How great is it to be able to do what you love," Kelsey said.

"Oh, I'm sorry, It's just, I still get excited about what I do." Jimmy shrugged.

"No, no. I love hearing about it. You're smarter than any of those people back home. You found what you like to do and by being partners in Big 4, you get to keep doing what you love. I also think you're a pretty smart guy. You don't give yourself enough credit. You should be proud of yourself. You're a great man, Jimmy."

She looked over at the napkin in her hand when he reached across the table and placed his hand on hers.

"Thanks. It means a lot to me coming from you, Kelsey. It really does."

They sat there staring into each others eyes until Jimmy said, "What about guys, you know, boyfriends? Bet there were lots of em?"

He saw her look down at her glass of wine while she played with the crystal stem. "I can only remember one guy who tugged at my heart strings. I was thirteen and he asked me to a school dance." She smiled at the memory. "Billy didn't like it."

"Who's Billy?" Jimmy asked.

"My oldest brother."

"I didn't know you had another brother. Is he trouble too?"

"Yes, Billy's trouble with a capital T. Although, he always took care of me. So much so he scared everybody off." She shook her head at the thought.

"Like the guy who wanted to take you to the dance?" Jimmy asked.

He noticed she nodded and went on, "His name was Gerald. He was a nice guy. I thought he was pretty cute too. Billy didn't think that way. He thought Gerald wanted something from me, ya know, sex. That wasn't true. Gerald never made a move on me. I did think I was going to get a kiss though, but I never got the chance because Billy came and took him out of the dance and gave him a black eye. And my brother just took me home. I hated my brother for a long time after what he did."

"If he was such a protector, why did he let Josh treat you like he did?"

"Billy never knew, at least I didn't think he did at the time. He moved out to California. He said it was the place to make his fortune." She shrugged.

"Did you ever tell him?" Jimmy questioned.

"Josh told me if I told Billy he'd kill me and I believed he would."

Jimmy could tell all this talk about her brothers was upsetting Kelsey so he took hold of her hand from across the table and asked, "Want to dance?"

Jimmy watched her look over at the couples dancing and nodded. So he lifted her up by her hand and before they knew it, they were in each others arms.

Kelsey was being held ever so tight. She didn't mind one bit because no one made her feel as safe as Jimmy did. All her problems were forgotten when he held her like this. She wanted to just close her eyes and stay cuddled in his warm embrace, although, she knew she couldn't do that and dance too. So she would make their dance do.

"You said you didn't date much but you're a good dancer." She smiled up at him.

"No, I didn't go out with girls. However, I had a teacher in 6th grade who made all us guys learn, girls too. It was one of the very few times as a young person I held a girl in my arms."

"Don't tell me you didn't date much later. You're a good lookin guy."

"Ya think I'm good lookin, huh?" He winked at her.

"Don't change the subject. Dates, Jimmy?"

"I really didn't date much until I got in with the guys at Big 4 and only because Bobby and Trent drove me nuts about it." He chuckled. "They felt I needed experience."

"Experience, huh? I assume you got it?"

"That, Kelsey, is personal and it has nothing to do with you and me." He cleared his throat.

She was enjoying how close Jimmy held her. They were so close she could feel his heart beating in his chest and she took a deep sigh at how she tingled at the closeness.

Kelsey was nervous so she whispered, "It just might have something to do with me. I don't have a lot of experience. You may not want a woman who you know, hasn't been with lots of guys."

A moment later she looked up at him because the music stopped and he led her back to the table where, she noticed, instead of sitting across from her as he did at dinner, he pulled a chair up next to her and placed his arm over the back of her chair.

Kelsey was taken aback by the change in his demeanor, though before she had a chance to worry about it, Jimmy handed her a glass of wine and took a sip of his. Suddenly chills went through her whole body. It was as if goose bumps covered her, all because he whispered in her ear.

"Kelsey, making love isn't a contest, it's a feeling two people have for one another. I've kissed you, touched you and when we both decide to go further it won't matter about experience."

She leaned close to him and spoke so only he could hear, "I saw first hand the kind of woman you like and frankly, I don't fit the bill."

"I told you, Tina and I are through and we are. How many times must I tell you? And my dear Kelsey, I'm not with Tina because she's not the kind of woman I want to be with, you are," he said with frustration in his voice.

"How can I be sure Jimmy?" She sounded worried.

She caught his frustration with her when he pulled money out of his pocket and threw one hundred and fifty dollars on the table, took hold of her hand and without a word he pulled her to the coat check window and with a few bucks for the girl, he held out her coat. She stared up at him with questioning eyes. However, Jimmy didn't answer those eyes. He just went right to buttoning her coat for her.

Before she knew it, she was sitting in his truck waiting for him to step in.

Once he did, she studied him as he sat back in his seat as he unbuttoned his double breasted jacket and looked across the truck at her.

"The date is over, isn't it?" she said with sadness in her voice.

"What's all this crap about Tina, Kelsey? Let me tell you something. I don't blow my hard earned money on girls I'm not interested in and for your information, I can get sex anywhere for a lot cheaper than what I just dished out!"

"Do you want me to pitch in some money?" She started going through her purse.

"It's not about the damn money!" he shouted.

Abruptly and without a clue she was pulled across the seat to him and her purse went flying. Before she could say a word Kelsey was snatched up close to him where he placed a kiss on her lips that nearly rendered her speechless. Remember, I said nearly. Because when he pulled away her eyes were closed, but she couldn't keep her mouth shut.

"I can see why Tina didn't want to lose you."

Her hair was nearly parted by Jimmy's deep breath which made her want to back away from him, although, all he did was unbutton her coat, grab hold of the coat lapels and pull her even closer. Kelsey didn't think it was possible. She found out it sure the hell was.

Her little black dress was tight up against his white dress shirt when he spoke with cool, calm, softness. "The subject of Tina is closed. We don't even think of her. You got it?"

She could tell by the sound of his voice this was serious to him. So she would have to try to forget about his ex-girlfriend and her worries.

Kelsey knew he didn't normally speak in that tone, in fact, she'd never heard him talk like this. She knew he must really be serious about being done with Tina. And by the way he spoke, if she didn't listen to him, he'd get rid of her, too, and she liked him far too much for that. She nodded.

After that, he pulled on the lapels of her coat so he could kiss her again. Lord help her she was soaring when he plunged his tongue into her mouth. Kelsey's mouth kept begging for more over and over and their lips went wild in total surrender.

It wasn't long before Jimmy knew he couldn't keep this up much longer without wanting to take her right there on the front seat of his pickup truck. He didn't think making love to her like this would be a good idea. With that thought in mind, he placed her on the seat, even gave her a peck on the lips.

He smiled as he looked at the contents of Kelsey's purse. They were now spread out all over the truck and he couldn't help but laugh.

"What's so funny?" she asked.

"You. Looks like you were looking for money to pay me."

"I was going to help you out…"

"Remember something, Kelsey, never try to pay the bill. If I take you out, I take you out. Ladies don't pay. And I was teasing you, because we were just talking about hookers." He could tell she was blushing because he could see how red her face was, even in the moonlight."

Once they were home, Jimmy stood at the door kissing Kelsey. He was determined to give her lots of time and space. He wanted her to tell him she wanted him and right now she was taking the lead.

After making out for twenty minutes, Jimmy gave her the biggest and longest kiss he'd ever given her. "Good night. I'll see you tomorrow. I really did have a good time," he told her.

"Yeah, me too," she agreed.

"Now lock your door." He kissed her forehead and left her there with her thoughts.

Kelsey closed the door, locked it, and leaned against it while she thought about Jimmy and those wonderful kisses. She remembered he never really made a move on her. She took her shoes off and carried them to the bedroom where she fell onto the bed thinking about Jimmy and the wonderful time they'd had together.

13

The next week was a busy one for Jimmy because Bobby and Benet took to the road covering for Trent who was busy taking care of his wife while they waited for the birth of their first child.

This left Jimmy in charge of not only watching the Big 4 office, but also fixing their trucks and there was Kelsey to worry about too. He was determined not to let her out of his sight. If he did he knew her brother would be there.

It was late Friday night when Jimmy came out of the garage and into the office wiping his freshly washed hands where he saw Kelsey filing some contracts into the cabinet. He was out of his coveralls, wearing jeans and a white Big 4 T shirt.

He noticed she was wearing a cute little short pleated black skirt with a white blouse and a black vest. He smiled at how much shorter the skirt got as she bent over. Damn, the view was great. He just sat on the corner of her desk enjoying the scenery.

"What?" She turned and caught him staring.

"Just enjoying the view." He shrugged.

"What view?"

He couldn't help but pull her close because she was standing right in front of him.

"You're the view, sweet thing and man I like what I see."

He loved the way Kelsey snuggled up close to him. However, he also knew he had to change the subject before he lost control.

"You have got to be hungry. It's nearly eight. You should have shouted for me. You know when I get into a job I lose all track of time."

"You were busy and I had stuff to do. I had to deal with Bobby and Benet today so my paperwork got put on the back burner." She shrugged.

"Bobby's having trouble with Trent's hauls?"

"Yeah, you know he wasn't on the road much until Candy's baby got so close. He's just not sure about time, deliveries, and places, so I had to walk him through it."

Jimmy nodded. He knew Bobby was a good driver but a much better salesman and that's where Big 4 needed him, at least until now.

"Come on, get your coat, let's go out to eat. I'd like to talk to you anyway. I know a great bar, actually it's Candy's bar, it's quiet and they have great food," he suggested.

"Okay, you're on." Kelsey jumped at the chance.

It wasn't long before they sat in a dark corner of the Scenic Bar and Grill. Jimmy was holding a long neck bottle of beer in his hand as Kelsey sipped on a Fuzzy Navel. The waitress had just taken their food order when they started to talk.

"So what did you want to talk about?" Kelsey asked.

"I wanted to talk to you about Josh."

"What about him?"

"I want you to let me take you to the police department and file papers against him," he said with seriousness in his voice.

"How can filing papers help me now? It'll only piss Josh off more than he is already!" She sighed.

Jimmy took hold of her hand across the table and she looked up at him.

"Listen, Kelsey, you need help with this if you ever expect to get your life back."

"Oh, I get it. You and the guys are tired of watching me. I understand, really I do, and I appreciate everything you guys have done for me."

"Kelsey, none of us is tired of anything. It's me who's asking you to put an injunction out on this guy. I'm worried. I don't want him hurting you again. An injunction will keep him away from you."

"And what if he won't stay away?" She sounded frightened.

"If he won't stay away, the cops will put him in jail for a long time," he assured her.

"I'm scared, Jimmy," she said as she looked deeply into his eyes.

"I know you are and that's why I'll go with you. We could do it tomorrow, if you like?"

"You're sure this is what I should do?" she asked.

"I'm not really sure of anything, but we have to do something. We just can't allow him to get away with this. I refuse to let him take your life, our life together away from us."

"Alright, I'll do it, if you'll go with me."

He held both her hands in his as he promised, "I'll do it. I'll be there with you. You're not alone in this, Kelsey."

The waitress set their plates down in front of them and Jimmy let the subject go for the moment. He knew she needed some time to get used to the idea and he'd give her that.

They were nearly done eating when Jimmy's cell phone rang. The caller ID said it was Trent, so he pressed the button.

"What's up, Trent? No kidding, really? We'll be there." Jimmy smiled over at Kelsey. "Candy's in labor and Trent sounds like a nervous wreck. We have to be there for him."

"Of course we do. I'm done, so if you are, let's go!"

The maternity waiting room was empty, except for Trent, who sat with his hands clasped between his knees. His head was down.

Jimmy had never seen his friend look so worried as Kelsey sat down beside him.

"How is she, Trent?"

"The doctor says since it's our first it could take a while," Trent told her.

Jimmy stood over him. "You look worried Trent. Is there a problem? Did the doctor say anything?"

"Hell, he's as cool as a cucumber, although I know a lot of things could happen."

"The doctor will tell you if there's a problem. They have to," Kelsey said as she patted his knee again.

"There's something more going on than you're telling us, isn't there?" Jimmy asked.

"Damn, I'm worried about Candice," Trent blurted out.

Jimmy saw Kelsey give him a confused look.

"He's talking about Candy. Trent doesn't like other guys calling her

Candy, but hell, we all do."

"Do you mind, Jimmy?" Trent said with frustration.

"Sorry, go on." Jimmy held his hands up in defense.

"I'm worried about the baby," Trent confessed.

"There's been no problem. Doctors know this stuff way ahead of time now," she assured him.

"No, Kelsey, it's not that. I'm going to be a father. I'm going to be responsible for another person's life. What if I make a mistake, one that could ruin the kid's life?"

All Jimmy did was laugh out loud.

"What's so damn funny, Jimmy? This is serious stuff."

"Listen, Trent, you've been taking care of people all your life. Hell, I was just a punk kid when you guys found me. Don't you remember how you set me on the right path?"

Jimmy leaned close to Trent. "You've also taught me a hell of a lot about women, too. And what about Candy's sisters? You stepped right in to be both brother and father to those girls. Out of the four of us guys at Big 4, you'll be the best dad. You were born to take care of people and frankly, Candy's the only woman I ever knew who could not only kick your ass, but make you love her too. So my friend, what's the problem?"

A moment later he saw Trent look down at Kelsey's hand on his knee and he patted it. "Ya know Kelsey, Jimmy here is a pretty smart and observant guy. If I were you I wouldn't let him get away."

"Yeah, he does have his good qualities, doesn't he?" She beamed up at him.

"Yes, he does," Trent said as he looked up at Jimmy. "You, kid, were worth all the trouble you gave me and thanks for the advice."

"Hey, aren't you supposed to be with your wife?" Jimmy asked.

"Yeah, I'm going now Would you guys stick around?"

"We planned on it," Kelsey answered before Jimmy could.

Jimmy stood there as Trent winked at Kelsey, gave him a one armed hug and left the room to be with his wife.

It was two in the morning when Jimmy's arm rested around Kelsey as they sat side by side in the waiting room hoping to hear about Trent's new baby. Kelsey was leaning against him sleeping while he thought about the mess with her brother.

He couldn't help but hope, once the police spoke with Josh, they would scare him away. Jimmy also knew that her brother wouldn't give up easily.

Suddenly the door burst open and Bobby walked in.

"How's Candy and how's Trent holding up?" he asked with concern.

"Shhh! Jimmy said in a loud whisper, "be quiet. Kelsey's trying to sleep." Bobby squatted down in front of them and whispered, "So?"

Jimmy continued the conversation in a loud whisper. "Everything is fine. Trent was just out here an hour ago. They expect the baby to make an appearance any time now."

Before they knew it both guys were surprised by another whispered voice.

"Hi Bobby,"

"Hey, Kelsey. Sorry I woke you up."

"I was only half asleep anyway." She rubbed her eyes.

"What in the hell are we whispering for?" Benet said as he stood there filling the doorway.

Jimmy spoke first, "Hey, I didn't think you two would be back until tomorrow."

"When we heard about Candy we decided to drive through the night," Bobby said.

Kelsey sat shaking her head and Benet gave her a funny look.

"What's the problem, Kelsey?" Benet asked.

"You guys. You're closer and care more about each other than people with the same blood. I think your unrelated family is the best.

Jimmy and the guys smiled at her. He knew her observation was spot on. There was no doubt in Jimmy's mind they were fortunate to have each other. They were also smart enough to guard their little family close to their hearts.

Just as the guys sat talking about their hauls, Trent walked in and everyone stared at him.

He grinned from ear to ear. "Well guys, we may want to rename the business in the future, to Big 5 because I have a 9 pound 4oz baby boy."

Kelsey and the guys jumped to their feet and hugged Trent and it wasn't long before they all followed him down the hall to the nursery where all 4 big, strapping guys made silly noises with their noses pushed up against the nursery glass.

Kelsey couldn't help but giggle at them because when she was done giggling she stood back and enjoyed all the love being bestowed on this little boy. She also knew she was fortunate to know these great guys.

14

Valentines Day had reared its lovely, snowy head and Kelsey was down stairs in the farmhouse kitchen making breakfast. She knew the smell of the fresh coffee would have the guys heading quickly down to the kitchen. She watched them come down the stairs, sniffing the air.

"I smell blueberry muffins," Bobby said.

"I smell bacon and eggs," Benet commented.

A few seconds later she saw Jimmy standing at the railing inhaling the air as he announced, "I smell cottage potatoes with onions."

Kelsey smiled when Bobby was the first one in. He was buttoning his blue dress shirt over his jeans. Benet entered next, dressed in jogging pants and a Big 4 T Shirt.

She shook her head when Jimmy came in last. He wore baggy jeans, and was sliding a red T Shirt over his head. They were a motley crew to be sure.

Kelsey wanted to laugh out loud when she saw them staring at the kitchen table. It was set for four. A pitcher of orange juice in the middle of the table along with a bowl of blueberry muffins, a plate of toast, scrambled eggs, bacon and cottage potatoes.

"Sit, eat, and happy Valentines Day," she announced.

She'd never seen the guys move so fast. In fact, they moved so quickly she giggled and poured the coffee as the guys filled their plates.

"I'm not complaining, mind you, but why the great breakfast?" Benet couldn't help, but ask.

Kelsey sat down and answered his question. "Two reasons. One, its Valentines day, and two, because you're all so good to me It's just my way of giving back, at least a little."

"You can thank me like this anytime, Kelsey. Yes, anytime at all," Bobby chimed in with a mouth full of food.

She watched the guys eat their fill, each giving her high praise indeed. Although, it wasn't long before Bobby and Benet were gone and only Kelsey and Jimmy remained.

She stared down at her half eaten muffin and said, "Do you have plans for tonight?"

Kelsey didn't notice that Jimmy sat back in his chair and waited to see if she'd look up at him. When she did he rewarded her with a smile.

"You know you're the only girl in my life."

"Well, you never said anything about Valentines Day." She acted shy.

"That's because I've worked late every night this week. Bobby's been bringing you home. So I haven't really had a chance to talk to you, now have I? I've been thinking about it, though, I thought maybe you and I could just have a quiet night right here. Have some Chinese, just be together. I told the guys to make plans to be gone."

"Jimmy, you can't kick those guys out of their own house."

"Look, Bobby is going to Trent's to play cards."

"Oh, Torrie's still home?" she said with a sweet little giggle.

"Yep, and Benet will be at the bar, looking for lonely girls on Valentines Day."

"Does that really work for him?"

"Oh, yeah," he said. And she gave the thought of Benet at the bar a big smile.

"Alright, Kelsey, what were you going to suggest?"

"I kind of had the same idea, only I thought I'd make a special dinner."

"Like what?" he prodded.

"Like a couple of great steaks, a baked potato and a salad. I thought I'd put you in charge of a good movie and you and I could cuddle up on the couch. Unless you'd rather have Chinese?"

"Okay, we'll go to the store this morning, get those steaks and whatever else strikes our fancy. I'll bring you back here. Although I have to go to work for a few hours. We'll meet back here at say… seven thirtyish?"

"I like it, Jimmy. We'll have fun."

Their eyes met, and Kelsey held her breath when he leaned over the table and graced her with a sweet kiss. Even the innocent kiss tingled her lips and left her wanting more.

Only Jimmy's next comment brought her back to reality.

"As long as you don't mind cooking, because we can always order out."

"No, I'm excited about cooking for you." She beamed.

"Alright, I'll help you clean up and we're out of here," he announced.

It was quarter after seven when Kelsey stood in the mirror looking at herself. She was wearing a red dress with a low cut neck-line which showed quite a bit of cleavage and a short flowing skirt which revealed plenty of leg.

Her short frosted hair was spiked on her head It looked perfect. A floating gold heart graced her neck. Little ones hung from her ears to finish off the whole look beautifully. She thought she looked good enough to be a Valentines Day present.

Kelsey smiled at her reflection. She decided tonight she would give herself to Jimmy. Heaven help her. This guy was for her and he wasn't going to slip through her fingers. The craziest thing about all of this was she really did want him. All she did was dream about him, even in the daylight. She was tired of dreaming, she wanted him for real.

Kelsey slipped on a pair of shiny red high heels, and went to light the candles on the table.

She stood back, a lit match still in her hand. When she looked around the flat, it was a wonderful romantic haven. A place where she hoped Jimmy would feel romantic too.

Kelsey was tossing the salad when she heard a knock. "Who is it?"

"Big 4, it's me, Jimmy." She ran to the door, only to stop before she opened it. Kelsey took a deep breath, smoothed down her dress and opened the door.

"Happy Valentines Day," is how she greeted him. Her smile widened when he handed her a dozen red roses, a heart shaped box of candy and a bottle of wine.

"Happy Valentines Day to you, too," and he kissed her.

"Thank you," she said softly, feeling heat in her face as she turned to the kitchen and placed the roses in a vase. She was happy she found an old dusty vase in the back of the cabinet.

She looked over and saw he'd followed her in and noticed the whole flat lit up in candlelight. She was hoping he wanted her as much as she wanted him.

Kelsey came out and set the roses on the coffee table along with the candy. When she looked up at him, he moved to her, put his hands around her waist and said, "Have I told you how great you look tonight? And everything here looks so romantic. Are you trying to tell me something?"

"Maybe I am. How about we save that for later, okay? I'm starving. How about you?" She hoped she sounded sexy.

"A steak, oh yeah, I could eat!" He rubbed his hands together with delight.

They spent most of the meal staring into each other's eyes until Kelsey began clearing the table. She was placing the dishes in the sink when she felt Jimmy's arms slide around her waist. His face was buried in her neck, kissing her, and she leaned back against him in blissful surrender.

"Man, Kelsey, you're killing me with the way you look tonight. I just can't keep my hands off you," he whispered as he nibbled on her ear.

"Oh, Jimmy, don't stop."

She sighed when he turned her around in his arms and gazed into her eyes. "Do you know what you're asking me? Do you know what will happen if I don't stop? We'll end up in your bed, Kelsey. I want you to be very sure of what you want."

"I do understand what will happen next, Jimmy. I love you, so there's no choice for me."

There was a sexy softness in her voice and eyes when she kissed him. Her lips seemed to hold him captive which left him wanting her, every inch of her.

She was still cuddled close to him when Jimmy took hold of her waist and walked her over to the couch where they sat next to each other.

"Kelsey, before we go any further I want you to know you're special to me."

Suddenly he slid something small out of his pocket and placed a little red velvet box in the palm of her hand. She stared at the box for what seemed like a long time.

"Open it," Jimmy encouraged.

The box squeaked open and revealed a two and a half carat Princess cut diamond ring. She just stared at it and he let her take it in. Kelsey needed to let it all soak in; he understood that about her.

Finally she smiled and he knew his patience had paid off because when she looked up at him, she said, "Does this mean what I think it means?"

"If you think it means I want to marry you, you're right. I'm in love with you too, so I have no choice. I think I fell in love with you the first time I watched you climb up on that big rig with no trouble. Yes, seems I've been in love with you for a while now. So, will you marry me?"

"Jimmy, are you sure, really sure?" This was important to her.

"Yes, and if you mention you know who, now, so help me, I'll ring your pretty little neck. This has nothing to do with anyone but us. So, will you marry me?"

She threw her arms around his neck and gave him a kiss that had him needing to touch her.

When Kelsey pulled away he took the ring from the box and placed it on the ring finger of her left hand

"It's a little big but we'll have it sized," he told her.

She nodded, kicked her shoes off and climbed into his lap. At that moment he couldn't help but slide his hand up her smooth leg as he laid claim to her lips. He had to have this girl, his girl, and tonight.

Jimmy was enjoying Kelsey's arms around his neck while she played with his ear and neck, and because of that, he had to kiss her. God, she was soft and had no stockings on. So when he slid his hand under her dress he felt her bottom and realized she had a thong on. The feel of her bare butt cheeks had him hot all over.

Lord help him, she was nibbling on his ear when he slid his hands between her soft thighs. He buried his head in her cleavage. Hellfire, he was ready to have her, be inside her right now.

At that precise moment he heard his cell phone ring. He ignored it. It no sooner stopped ringing, than it rang again. His breath was ragged with desire when he pulled the phone out of his breast pocket. The caller ID read, Trent. He looked into her eyes. "It's Trent, he's on the road. I have to take this."

She nodded and they both knew if Trent called Jimmy, there was a problem.

"Yeah, man," he answered.

All Jimmy did was agree, until he slipped the phone back into his pocket. "I've got to go. Trent's stranded on the interstate. I can't leave him there."

"I know, it's just bad timing." Kelsey slid her hand down his chest.

"No shit!" And they were both smiling. "Look, I'll go take care of Trent. I'll be back by midnight. Will you wait for me?"

"You know I will," she whispered.

Jimmy headed for the door leading down into the rest of the house.

"No, your car's out back. Take the outside stairs."

"I'm not taking the bar down," he told her.

"No, look, Benet said spring's coming, so he put a bunch of locks on it. He said I could use it while keeping it locked," she explained.

"Alright, walk me to the railing."

She slid her shoes on and walked him outside to the railing of the small deck three floors up.

They stood in the cold February wind as Jimmy kissed her goodbye. He held her tight as her red dress whipped around her thighs. At that moment, neither one thought they'd be saying goodbye so soon.

With one more kiss, he said, "Now, get in there, I'm not leaving until I hear all three locks click shut."

"Okay Jimmy." She went inside and did just that.

Kelsey leaned against the back door and stared at the sparkling square diamond ring on her hand. She was getting married to the man she loved. Looking up to the heavens, she said, "Thanks for letting me work for Big 4 and those great guys but mostly for giving me a man I love and who loves me."

The dishes were all clean and put away when Kelsey sat on the couch picking at her candy. She heard a knock at the back door. Immediately she thought Jimmy was back, but was he?

Kelsey went to the door with excitement, but at that moment she remembered all the safety tips her bosses had given her. Even Benet told her to never even trust his locks, be cautious and think safety. His words rang in her ears. So she approached the door cautiously, opened the lace curtain, and she jumped back.

"Let me in, Kelsey, or you'll be sorry!" the voice shouted.

She screamed from ten feet away from the door. "Get out of here, Josh, I've filed papers against you!"

"Yeah, I know. Cops came to my door and served me those damn papers. Bitch, I can't believe you'd do such a thing to your own brother."

"All I want from you is to get out of my life!" Tears rolled down her cheeks.

"Yeah, I see you got you a man now. But hell, Kelsey, no one can be with you every minute." He snickered.

"That's what the papers are for. If you don't get out of here now, Josh, I'm calling the cops!"

"Go ahead, and so help me, Kelsey, I'll kill you," Josh roared.

Suddenly she froze at the sound of the door being kicked in. She panicked, but all she could do was step back as she watched the wood from the door splinter everywhere.

In that instant Kelsey tried to remember what the guys told her. So she ran for the bedroom, Josh in hot pursuit.

She had the fancy scented oil bottle behind her back when her brother entered the room. Kelsey was backing away from him. She nearly made it to the bed when her brother grabbed her arm. That was unexpected. So she dropped the heavy bottle of oil on the floor and it shattered into a million pieces.

Kelsey pulled her arm out of his grasp, while Josh tried to figure out what had just happened. She rolled over the bed and took hold of the truck tire iron Benet had given her.

"If you don't get the hell out of here, so help me I'll smash your skull in!" she shouted as she showed him the tire iron. However, all her brother did was laugh at her.

It was then Kelsey realized she was shaking. How could she put on a good front, if her hands continued to shake like this?

Now she was afraid, because Josh reaffirmed what she was thinking when he said, "Look at you. You don't have the guts to do something like that. You're just a scared little girl."

Kelsey could now hear Trent's voice in her ears. "Even if you're so scared you don't think you can do it, put on a hard face. Half the battle is making your opponent think you mean every word you say. You have to convince him you will do exactly what you say you will. For the love of God, act the part!"

It was as though she was willing her body to cooperate with the look on her face because now she stood straight and tall, defiant even. The look of her made Josh take a step back. She hoped he saw something different about her because she wanted him to know she would fight back this time. Yes, his sister was no longer an easy prey, and damn if she didn't look as if she would crack his skull open.

Kelsey watched him shake his head.

"I need the money," he said.

"Can't you see I'm sweating and shaking? I need another fix. Right now, I don't know how I'm going to get the fix, but I'll be damned if I don't get the money from you," he roared.

She knew there would be no changing his mind, because Josh headed straight for her. It was as if he knew he had to move fast if he wanted to get the tire iron out of her hand.

Before he did, she got in one good whack and she heard a bone in his arm snap, followed by his scream of pain. He yanked the tire iron out of her hand, and she stepped back as he shouted, he was going to kill her with the damn thing.

Kelsey scrambled back over the bed trying not to step on the shards of glass. She was screaming with pain when she ran barefoot out of the room and into the living room. She didn't get far before he caught her and slapped her in the face. He hit her so hard she fell backwards onto the couch, where he knelt over her.

"You know, sis, I'm going to kill you. There has to be some cash around here and you owe me double after breaking my damn arm!"

"She doesn't owe you shit, Josh!"

They both knew the voice; it was Billy.

Kelsey watched Josh go sailing across the room in what seemed like slow motion.

"I'm going to tell ya once, and only once, get the hell out of here, Josh. If

I ever find out you've come after our sister again, you'll be signing your own death warrant," Billy yelled.

"You wouldn't kill your own brother?" Josh whined .

"I've killed before and you know it, and believe me, when I get done with you, Kelsey here won't even be able to identify your body." Billy grabbed hold of his brother's shirt.

Kelsey watched in fear as Billy flipped open his switchblade, and Josh backed away, his hands in the air.

"Now, get the hell out of here, now Josh!" Billy shouted.

She saw Josh head for the door, and Billy turned his attention to Kelsey. He leaned over her on the couch. "Are you okay? Do you need a doctor?"

There wasn't even enough time for Kelsey to warn Billy when Josh came up behind him.

She just pulled the truck wrench from the couch cushion and slapped it into Billy's hand. She knew at that moment Josh was trying to kill him, and when she put the wrench in Billy's hand, he knew too. Billy jerked around and hit Josh in his bad arm, and his brother hit the floor in agony.

"Damn it, Josh, I told you to get the hell out of here. You're not going to be happy until I kill you, are you?" Billy hollered.

"I need the money, Billy, and she owes me," Josh said between moans.

"How does Kelsey owe you? She's not your personal ATM. And I also talked to the pretty little woman who hired you."

"Tina, you talked to Tina?" Josh sounded panicked.

"Yeah, and the conversation was very interesting. Seems she heard a lot about you and our sister. Her friend told her you did lots of bad things to Kelsey when you were supposed to be taking care of her. You were using her for your meal ticket. You even made Tina believe you had control over her, your own sister!"

Kelsey interrupted their conversation. "Not Tina—not Jimmy's old girlfriend, Tina?" She couldn't believe it.

"Yep, one in the same. She found out how sick Josh here was so she hired him to get you out of town. Little did she know what a problem he had. Yeah Josh, I know you have a monkey on your back, and as long as you do, you'll never live a good life," Billy insisted.

"Look who the hell is talking? Don't think I don't know what you've done with your life," Josh shouted.

"Hey man, I've worked as a lineman, laid pipe lines, even drove trucks. I admit I've also taken a little shady work now and again. But I never, I mean never, hit a woman. As far as I'm concerned, Josh, you've broken a cardinal rule, two actually, one striking a woman, and two, a woman of your own damn blood!" Billy declared.

She saw Josh struggle to his feet, holding his broken arm against his body.

"Take your sorry ass out of here, and I promise you, if I ever hear you've touched a hair on Kelsey's head, I'll hunt you down like a dog, just to kill ya!" Billy told him.

Again, Kelsey and Billy made a mistake trusting their brother, Josh, when he stepped away from them because once they turned their backs, Josh headed for the truck wrench on the floor. Only seconds later Billy's body hit the floor, blood seeping from his head.

Kelsey found herself staring at the blood flowing from her brother's head. Time seemed to slow to a snail's pace. Breathing became difficult and her eyes welled up with tears. Was her oldest brother dead?

Slowly she regained her wits as she looked over at Josh. There was pure hatred in her eyes, although by the expression on Josh's face she knew he wasn't feeling one bit of remorse. All she saw was anger in his eyes; he'd ceased having any conscience, or even fear. It was apparent he needed a fix but she wasn't going to give it to him. By the way he was approaching her, she also understood he didn't even feel the pain from his broken arm anymore.

A moment later he tried to take full advantage of the far away look in Kelsey's eyes. But, once he touched her she came out of it because he grabbed hold of her and tried to take her out of the flat.

Kelsey had a history with Josh, knew him well. If he got her out of her flat she'd never see it or Jimmy again. He had hold of her right arm so she slapped his face with all the power she could muster with her left and blood poured down his cheek. Josh touched the deep gouge in his skin. His fingers were full of blood.

She almost made it to the door and Josh was convinced she was running from him. However, it was really the bat by the door she wanted. It didn't matter though, because he caught hold of her hand and yanked her to a stop.

Kelsey was jerked around and her brother opened her left hand, and looked down at her palm. There it was, the stone of her engagement ring; it was large, and so was the gold band setting. The stone was so big it had slid around her finger to the inside of her hand. She watched him grin at the size of the diamond. Kelsey figured he was now counting the money he could get from her ring in his head. She closed her hand as Josh reached for the ring.

"You'll take this ring over my dead body!" she screamed.

"That can be arranged, sister," he snarled.

As she struggled to keep her new engagement ring her fingers of her other hand were stretching to grab hold of the bat. She was in a panic because she knew the bat was her last hope. Trent's voice kept echoing in her ears. "Hit him out of the ball park!"

Kelsey kept pulling her hand away from his grasp as he struggled to take her ring. Finally the palm of her right hand covered the top of the bat. She was close. One more step away from Josh and she would be choking the neck of the bat.

They struggled around the kitchen as Kelsey tried to get a good grip on the bat that was now behind her back. She knew if he saw it and she didn't have a good grip on it, he'd take it from her for sure. But right now she understood all Josh was thinking of was the gold mine on her finger. His eyes were wide, frightening and blood shot. She thought he looked more like a madman every moment and it seemed to frighten her even more.

Back at the Big 4 office. Jimmy had just come back with Trent's bad part. He was making himself a note to order another one, but his mind was on Kelsey and spending some special time with her. So, once he was finished, he locked the door and headed for his truck.

He turned the key and the engine wouldn't turn over. The steering wheel took an angry blow from Jimmy's fist. Why was he having this problem when he just drove to the interstate and back?

Jimmy decided he would let it go. It was time to get back to Kelsey, and out the door he went to find out what was wrong with his truck.

Hell, it took him several minutes to put the wire harness back on the motor. How in God's name did that happen? It was almost like someone had pulled it off when he was in the garage. Jimmy shook his head at the crazy idea. Why would anyone mess with his truck in the middle of the night?

All of a sudden his thoughts went to Kelsey, he couldn't help it. Because this thing with his truck seemed pretty strange. Yet, there was no doubt in his mind she was safe and sound. He heard her lock herself in before he left. Jimmy took a deep breath, yes she was fine, but he was still going to hurry home just the same. Nothing was going to happen to her. She was going to be his wife.

While brother and sister struggled in the upper flat, Jimmy had just pulled up at the back stairs leading to the 3rd floor. He was determined to make sure Kelsey was safe. He couldn't help but smile, because tonight, they would finally be together.

Jimmy started up the back steps when he heard Kelsey scream. Looking up at the struggling shadows he saw through the kitchen window made his heart jump into his throat. Pure panic set in.

He took two and three steps at a time up the stairs. Midway up them he saw the splintered door when it burst open and Josh and Kelsey's fight now raged on the small back landing. He watched in horror as Josh struggled to get Kelsey's ring off her finger; he could see she was just as determined not to give it up.

Jimmy stilled as he watched Kelsey being pushed from side to side on the landing and nearly stopped breathing, praying she wouldn't fall over the railing.

"Give me the ring Kelsey, or so help me I'll kill you!" Josh shouted.

"I'll never give you this ring, never!" she screamed back.

Jimmy started up the stairs again, hoping neither one of them saw him coming. He didn't think they did because they continued to struggle. Jimmy was nearly to them when he heard Kelsey shout again, "You'll never have this ring, never!"

At that moment he saw Josh put his hands around her neck. She was being held over the porch railing three stories in the air. Jimmy lost his control, and yelled, "Damn it Kelsey, give him the infernal ring!"

Jimmy knew his words had Josh's full attention and he pulled away from Kelsey. He was now facing Jimmy who was ready to deal with him and that's when Josh turned the whole situation around. "If you come any closer, I'll throw her off this porch!"

"For God's sake, she's your sister. You'd kill your own sister?" Jimmy shouted.

"Family means nothing to me," Josh yelled.

Jimmy watched in fear as Josh turned on Kelsey. But this time, she was waiting for him because before he could even think, she hit her brother with the Louiville slugger, right in his mid section. He roared with pain, only to lose his footing and tumble down three long flights of stairs. Jimmy had to jump onto the railing so he wouldn't be plowed over.

Jimmy saw Kelsey lean over the porch rail and they both watched Josh hit the ground at the same time. Her brother let out an ear piercing scream of pain and everything went silent. He was lying in a heap at the bottom of the stairs.

That was all the attention Jimmy gave Josh because then he hurried straight to Kelsey. A moment later he was holding her in his arms.

"I killed my own brother." She sobbed.

"He would have killed you without a second thought. You did what you had to do, Kelsey," Jimmy soothed.

A moment later Billy staggered out of the flat and onto the back porch. He held a white kitchen towel to his head. It was soaked with bright red blood.

"I'm sorry, Kelsey. I couldn't get to you in time," Billy said with regret in his voice.

"Who's this?" Jimmy asked.

"He's my brother, Billy. He was trying to get Josh to leave. He almost succeeded until Josh hit him in the head with the wrench you gave me," Kelsey explained.

"What happened? Is Josh dead?" Billy asked as he looked over the side of the deck

Jimmy answered his question. "Kelsey hit him in the gut with a bat and down he fell. I was too worried about Kelsey to check."

Jimmy and Kelsey stood together while Billy, who was still holding the blood soaked towel to his head, made his way down the steps to his brother on the ground, where he took his pulse.

"He's alive. But, by the looks of him, he's pretty broke up," Billy shouted up.

Silence fell between the three of them for long moments until Billy headed back up the steps where he stood in front of his sister.

"Is this the famous Jimmy?" Billy asked with a grin.

"I don't know about famous, but he's my Jimmy." And she reached her hand out to show him her engagement ring.

Jimmy saw him smile at her. "So you finally found a good guy, you deserve it, sis," Billy said as he looked up at Jimmy.

"You better take care of her. I'll be watching," Billy told him.

Jimmy turned the subject just a little. "What did you mean when you called me famous?"

"You didn't know? Your friend Tina hired Josh to get Kelsey here out of town. She wanted you back."

Jimmy shook his head. "That wasn't going to happen. I told her it was over between us and it had been for a long while. I'm in love with Kelsey, been that way since I saw her the first time. Tina had this wrong. I was never going back to her."

"I don't think she'll be giving you anymore trouble. Josh took her last penny. Billy informed him.

She almost got Kelsey killed," Jimmy blurted out.

"Yeah, but in all honesty, she only hired Josh because he promised to get you out of town, Kelsey. She told me she didn't think Josh would ever hurt his own sister." Billy shrugged.

Jimmy was shaking his head at the whole damn mess when he said, "I'm gonna call the police."

"If you call the police, I'll go to jail," Kelsey said as she grabbed hold of his arm.

He gave her a sweet smile and held her face in his hands. "You didn't do anything wrong, sweet thing, it was self defense, and Josh went against the injunction, too. No, he's gonna spend a long time in jail."

"And once they find the coke in his car, they're gonna put him away until he's old and gray," Billy added.

"And Kelsey, he tried to not only rob you, but take your life. He'll have a lot of explaining to do," Jimmy insisted.

Once more they all looked down at Josh still lying in a heap at the foot of the stairs. There was nothing to be done about him. They knew in their hearts, Josh did this to himself.

Once Jimmy went inside to call the police, Billy gave Kelsey a big hug.

"The cops are comin, ya know I can't stay, there's paper on me, sis," he insisted, as she hugged her brother hard.

"Why is our family so screwed up? Josh is a psycho and you're always running from the cops. Will I ever see you again?" she said with tears in her eyes.

"Yeah, Kelsey, you'll see me again. I'll come back this way again sometime. Maybe by then you'll have ten kids, but I'll be back. You're my baby sister." He kissed her cheek and with a smile he headed down the stairs.

"What do I tell the police?" she yelled down to him.

"Ya do what's right, sis, you tell the truth."

"What about you being here and the fight with Josh?" she asked.

"I didn't do anything wrong, just tried to help my sister." He waved and down the stairs and into the night he went.

15

The sun was beginning to come up when the last policemen finished with his questions.

Jimmy was tired, but Kelsey couldn't keep her eyes open. He knew it was because she'd been answering questions all night.

They were both holding each other when Jimmy closed and locked the door he'd just fixed behind them and turned his attention to Kelsey and gave her a gentle squeeze.

"It's done with Kelsey. The police officer told me Josh would be put away until he's an old man. He tried to kill you, assaulted you, and with the papers we filed against him, it's pretty cut and dry. So you can put this all behind you now," he explained.

Jimmy pushed her away and looked into her eyes. They were filled with tears. "Aw, sweet thing, I told you, it's done with."

"I'm not crying because I'm worried about Josh coming after me. No, it's because it's finally over, I'm free, thanks to you and Big 4. I can finally sleep without fear of Josh. For the first time in my life, I can look forward to the future."

Jimmy interrupted her. "Yes, Kelsey, a future with me, a family of our own. He's out of our lives and that's where he'll stay."

Again he had her in his arms where he could feel the tenseness in her body fade away. He couldn't help but smile because he knew right there and then, Kelsey was going to be a happier person.

Without a word he lifted her into his arms. She was exhausted and so was he. Jimmy carried her to the bedroom and laid her on the bed. He'd just finished cleaning up the glass that had shattered from the body oil on the floor in her fight with Josh and now he was going through her drawers until he found a night gown He pulled out a short, light blue gown out and handed it to her. "Put this on." Then he leaned close and emphasized, "now!"

"You're watching" She wouldn't look at him.

"Yeah, and so what, we're getting married, Kelsey." He grinned.

"Yeah, but not just yet." she informed him.

Jimmy took a deep cleansing breath, folded his arms across his chest and turned around. "Okay, hurry up and get on with it!"

He figured she had never gotten undressed so quickly in her life. Only moments later she stood in front of him, undressed, and in her short nightie.

"I'm ready for bed, you can go now," she said.

Jimmy's only answer was to step over to the other side of the bed, pull his boots off, unbutton his shirt and unbuckle his belt. He pulled the leather strap through the pant loops, and before she knew it, he was stretched out on the bed. His hands clasped behind his head, just smiling at her.

"Get in bed here next to me, Kelsey."

"This isn't right, Jimmy." She shook her head slowly at him.

"For God sakes, we were going to make love only a few hours ago." He couldn't hide the frustration in his voice.

"But Jimmy…"

"Look Kelsey, I'm not going to make you do anything you don't want to. And hell, we're both exhausted. I want you to have all your energy when we finally come together, so get in the damn bed!" he ordered.

Jimmy wanted to laugh at the way she shyly slid into bed. He swore once she was in as she teetered on the edge.

So without warning he pulled her over to him where he cradled her in his arms. He could feel her tremble so he pulled up the quilt at the end of the bed and covered them both, only to rest his chin on her head.

"Good night, Kelsey."

"Night, Jimmy."

He lay awake until he felt her completely relax in his arms and he closed his eyes, thinking all about how he would make slow passionate love to Kelsey, yes, slow and easy, until she begged him for more.

All of a sudden he felt her bottom press up against his hard arousal. Lord, he was too tired for this so he found himself trying to think of a truck he was working on. Anything, but Kelsey's butt. He fell asleep fixing a transmission in his head.

Kelsey didn't wake until nearly one the next afternoon to the smell of fried potatoes, bacon, eggs and toast She smiled herself awake.

She slid out of bed and hurried to the bathroom where she freshened up, washed her face and brushed her teeth. She was still wearing the same short little blue nightie when she slowly walked into the kitchen. Jimmy's back was to her. How nice, he was making breakfast. She sighed.

"Is there enough for me?" she asked.

She saw him turn around with a smile on his face. "There sure in the hell is."

Kelsey gave him a sweet grin when he took hold of her hand, led her to a kitchen chair and she sat down. She took a deep breath when Jimmy placed a sweet kiss on her lips and said, "Damn, you look good in the morning!"

"So do you," she said shyly.

For some reason she felt strange. She couldn't seem to shake the sight of her brother's broken body at the bottom of the stairs.

Jimmy was still staring at her from across the room. God, she looked wonderful, but he could see she was deep inside herself. He didn't like that one bit.

"I hope you like scrambled eggs, potatoes and crisp bacon."

He didn't know she hadn't heard him because the truth was, she hadn't. She was still deep inside her mind. So he just placed a plate full of food in front of her and stooped down next to her chair.

"Look at me, Kelsey."

He noticed she was still staring off when he took hold of her chin until she was looking into his eyes.

"Do you know who I am?" He was encouraged because she favored him with a beautiful smile.

"Of course I do, you're Jimmy."

Jimmy studied her as she looked down at the beautiful engagement ring on her finger. "You're going to be my husband."

He never let go of her chin, just pulled her closer and placed a very sexy kiss on her lips, a deep arousing kiss, one which promised much more. When he pulled away, her lips were red and a bit swollen from his kiss, only the passion still lingered in her eyes.

Afterwards, Jimmy gave her chin a gentle squeeze to get her attention again. When she looked up into his eyes, he said, "Eat, you need your strength." He winked at her. "You're going to need it because very soon we're gonna finish where we left off last night."

Once he looked into her eyes, he knew she understood exactly what he was promising. He smiled because Kelsey gave him her very first wink and she dug into the eggs.

Jimmy hoped she wanted his promise to come true. And with the way she was eating, Jimmy knew she wanted what he did. A few moments later he sat across the table from her. A knife in one hand a fork in the other cutting his bacon.

"There's something I want to talk to you about." He took a big sip of his black coffee and went on. "We both want to get married, don't we?"

She wiggled her ring finger at him, her mouth full of potatoes.

"You're not getting out of this Jimmy, yes, we're getting married."

He leaned across the table. "I, Kelsey, have no intention of getting out of this. Nor do I plan to let you take back your word to me. Hell no! My only question is, how fast can we get this done?" She was cutting her eggs when the motion stilled.

"You act like our wedding is an inconvenience."

"I don't mean that at all." He reached across the table and placed his hand on hers. "I'm just really anxious for you to be mine."

He went back to his breakfast as he said, "I have no intention of letting you spend another night here alone. Married, or not, it's you and me together, so the sooner we make it legal, the better."

"Do I have anything to say about this?" she asked.

"You took my ring, sweet thing, you're mine!

"Is this what I'm going to have to deal with my whole life?" she questioned.

He took a bite of his toast, talking at the same time.

"Probably."

"What have I gotten myself into?" She shook her head at him.

The chuckle he gave her next made her giggle. He was truly a crazy man, but there was no hiding the fact she loved him, it was there in her eyes. He could see she liked the teasing banter between them. Jimmy hoped Kelsey would enjoy it for the rest of her life and never tire of it because he knew he wouldn't.

A moment later, he lifted her off the chair. Jimmy had her in his arms and he started towards the bedroom when Trent, Bobby and Benet stormed in. Jimmy could do nothing but take a ragged breath.

"Bobby just told Benet and I what happened last night, are you both okay?" Trent started off.

Jimmy didn't answer him immediately. He just carried Kelsey to the bedroom door, placed her on her feet and said, "Why don't you get dressed, and I'll talk to the guys." Kelsey placed a gentle kiss on his lips and he closed the door behind her.

He turned to his partners and they all started talking at the same time, until Jimmy shouted, "Sit down all of you, and I'll explain everything."

Jimmy told the guys the full story as he knew it. Once he finished the questions began.

"How's Kelsey taking this? Hell, Josh is her brother after all?" Trent was the first to ask.

Jimmy shrugged. "She won't admit it but I think the events of last night are weighing pretty heavily on her."

"So, the weapons we gave her helped?" Benet asked.

"I'll tell you Benet, if she hadn't had them, he may have killed her, or surely beat her again."

"He didn't get a lick in, did he?" Bobby said as Benet nodded his head in agreement.

Jimmy took a deep breath. "I won't lie to you. She's got a few bruises, but nothing too bad at all."

"How in the hell would you know about her bruises. You better not have taken advantage of that poor girl's situation," Trent said as he stepped forward.

Jimmy roared, "Please...!"

At that moment, Kelsey came out of the bedroom. She was wearing tight jogging pants and a fitted short sleeved shirt. With hands on her hips, she smiled.

Kelsey heard Trent's remark and had to show him something. So she stood in the middle of all the guys and wiggled the third finger of her left hand in their faces. "Jimmy and I are engaged."

Kelsey was literally pushed out of the way so the guys could congratulate Jimmy. She couldn't help but shake her head at these guys she'd come to care for so much. They were more of a family to her than her real family. That wonderful thought made her happy.

Suddenly she was bombarded by Trent, Bobby and Benet. They lifted her up into their arms and threw her around like a beach ball. Each one hugged her and welcomed her into their tight knit Big 4 family.

It wasn't long before Jimmy pulled her away from his partners and into his arms.

"We'll have the wedding at our house. Candy loves a party and she sure in the hell likes you, Kelsey," Trent said.

"I don't know, Trent. The baby's only a few months old. It may all be too much for her. Jimmy and I can just go to the justice of the peace." Kelsey argued.

"The hell you will!" Trent shouted.

"I have a friend who's a preacher," Bobby interrupted.

Jimmy saw Kelsey look up at him.

"Doesn't it seem like Bobby knows someone in every profession?" Kelsey asked.

"It's a good idea to be nice to everyone because you never know when you just might need a little help." Bobby's warm chuckle filled the room.

Jimmy was amazed when Bobby pulled his cell phone out of his jean pocket and pushed in some numbers. Yep, his partner knew everyone, their numbers too.

"I'll find out when he can do it. What's a good time for you?" Bobby inquired.

"Preferably now," Jimmy announced. And all the guys laughed out loud.

A few moments later Jimmy watched Bobby walk back into the room, he was still talking on the phone. "He says he can marry you two on Sunday."

"Sunday, tomorrow's Sunday?" Benet said.

Jimmy jumped at it. "Works for me!" A second later everyone was staring at Kelsey and in unison, said, "So…?"

"Tomorrow…?" She looked Jimmy in the eye.

He didn't want to talk to her in front of his partners so he took hold of her hand, dragged her into the bedroom and closed the door behind them.

Jimmy sat down on the end of the bed, pulling her down with him. He took a deep breath and looked into her eyes. "I know I love you, Kelsey, but the question is, do you love me?"

"I do, Jimmy. I think I have from the beginning," she said in a soft voice.

He placed his hand on hers and she looked up at him. "The question is, do you love me enough to marry me tomorrow?"

"I'll marry you whenever you like. I can't help it. I'm yours and have been for a long time."

Leaning down, smiling, he took her warm mouth in a deep sexual kiss that not only had his body reacting, but had her thoughts completely scrambled. Funny, but she didn't even care.

It wasn't long before they emerged from the bedroom. Kelsey was at his side, his arm anchored her shoulders as he announced, "Tomorrow it is!"

A moment later all three guys were on their cell phones.

"Candice says you're to come home with me, something about shopping," Trent informed her.

"I knew I liked Candy from the very beginning," Kelsey said with a big grin.

"I'm taking her to my house, Jimmy," Trent laughingly said as he took Kelsey's hand. "She and Candy are going wedding shopping."

Jimmy immediately took hold of her other hand and snatched her back to him.

"Jimmy, I'm not taking her away for life." Trent shot him a confused look.

"Just give us a minute," Jimmy barked as he led her into the kitchen.

"You are really okay with this, aren't you?" he whispered.

All of a sudden his worries flew out the window when she placed a sweet kiss on his lips.

"Yes, tomorrow I'll be your wife, and I really would like to look wonderful for you."

He reached into his pocket. "Do you need money?"

"Nope, I've got it covered." She beamed up at him.

"Okay, I'll see you later." She kissed him again and said, "Later!"

Jimmy didn't hear from Kelsey again until he received a call at ten p.m. that night.

"Finally, I was beginning to worry about you." He sounded agitated.

"I'm sorry, Jimmy, I didn't mean to worry you. We've just been running all over, trying to get everything we need for the wedding. Don't worry though, our wedding is going to be just perfect."

"I didn't have any doubt, as long as we're both there, I'm good."

"You're really easy to please, aren't you?"

"Yes, ma'am, all I want is you, now. When are you coming home?"

"Well, Jimmy..."

"I don't like the sound of this."

"Candy and I were talking. She thinks I should stay here tonight. Seeing we're getting married so early tomorrow, this way I'll have plenty of time to get ready."

"Kelsey, I thought you and I were going to get together tonight."

"I know Jimmy, but can't we wait one more night, please?"

He sighed and she held her breath. Jimmy knew this wasn't about hurting him. It was about their wedding, so he decided to let her enjoy it.

"Okay, Kelsey, but this is your very last reprieve. Tomorrow we do this my way."

"And I'll be awfully happy to oblige you."

"You better be," he warned.

"You can count on a wonderful wedding night." She giggled.

"Sweet dreams, Kelsey."

"Good night and dream of me," she whispered.

"That won't be hard at all."

"Love ya." She sighed.

"Yeah, me too," he said.

16

It was bitter cold on their wedding day, and Kelsey woke to the sight of large white snowflakes falling outside the bedroom window. They were filling the ground rapidly.

She sat on the bed in Candy's sister Torrie's room, thinking how today was her wedding day. She sat Indian style on the bed, just staring at the snowflakes.

Her thoughts were of Jimmy. Kelsey smiled as she pictured their first meeting. He was straddling the engine of a big rig. Her heart rate quickened at the very thought of him. Yeah, this guy was for her, there was no mistake about it. Never did she think she would get married. She didn't think this kind of happiness was meant for her. Thank God for Jimmy and she looked up into the sky and offered a prayer for him.

"Thank you, dear Lord, for sending Jimmy to me. He makes me feel loved and desired. Oh, and I'm so glad you didn't forget about me."

Kelsey had spoken the last word of her little prayer when the door opened. There stood Candy, a baby in her arms.

Kelsey couldn't help but smile. After spending the day with Candy yesterday, she felt a sisterly closeness to her. This lovely lady would do anything for her, and Kelsey treasured their friendship.

"Good morning, bride," Candy said.

"I am the bride, aren't I?" Her eyes sparkled with the thought.

"Yep, you should come and have something to eat because you're going to have a very busy day," Candy told her.

Kelsey placed her hand on her belly. "Ya know, I haven't eaten since breakfast yesterday."

"Oh my goodness, you better eat something, Trent's making pancakes and sausages, c'mon."

Kelsey placed her arms through Torrie's robe, messed her hair up and said, "I'm ready."

"I wish I had the confidence to wear such an easy hair style." Candy shook her head.

Kelsey giggled as she said, "It's all in the wrists."

Fifteen minutes later, Kelsey and the Kelly family sat at the kitchen table eating pancakes. She was listening to Candy go on about the wedding menu, which her own bar was catering, when there was a knock at the door and Candy hurried to answer it.

Once she was out of the room, Kelsey saw Trent lean over the table to her. "I hope you don't mind. I know Candy's kind of running the show but she's having so much fun, I didn't have the heart to remind her, this is your wedding."

"Don't give it a second thought. I think of Candy like a sister, never had one, and I really am blessed with her help, especially since Jimmy can't get married fast enough."

"Do you know why that is?" Trent gave her a devilish smile.

She shrugged. "I guess it's the sex thing."

"Yeah, I'm sure it is the sex, although I wouldn't put it quite that way." Trent chuckled.

"Oh, don't get me wrong, I think he cares for me. But you see, we have this sex thing going on."

"Sex thing?" He raised an eyebrow.

"Yeah, we have both been trying to put it out of our minds and we just can't manage it." She sighed.

Kelsey didn't realize Trent knew exactly what she was talking about because he felt the very same way about his wife, and if the truth was known, he still did.

"I get the sex thing, I'm a man, although, I don't get you." He pointed at her.

Kelsey took a big sip of coffee and explained. "Of course Jimmy got me thinking about the sex stuff. However, I have another motivation."

"And what's that?" Trent wanted to hear this.

"I happen to love the grease monkey, so for me it's the right thing to do."

"You don't think Jimmy loves you?" He looked suspicious.

She shrugged. "He says he does."

"You don't believe him?"

"Oh, I believe he cares for me, but love, I'm not really certain."

She sat with her coffee, watching as Trent stared at the pile of pancakes in the middle of the table.

"Ya know, Kelsey, men are funny creatures. They'll lay between a woman's legs and have sex with her all night long, only to walk away the next morning with a smile on their faces, and never see the girl again. Sex is just sex. However, when a man tells a woman he loves her, you can bet a month's salary he's telling the truth. Because for a man to love you, he has to admit to himself and you, it isn't all about sex. I know Candy brought it all out in me. And before I knew it, I had a family, and damn if I'm not a happy man," he said as he held his coffee in both hands.

Kelsey smiled at him. "So you think there's hope for me and Jimmy?"

"Oh, hell yeah!"

She leaned over the table and hugged his neck as she whispered, "Thanks, Trent, I think I understand."

"Good, now let's get this over with so I can have my house back." He grinned at her.

Kelsey jumped to her feet. "You got it!" And she ran through the kitchen door, into the living room where she began talking to Candy.

Kelsey was helping Candy wrap some silverware when she overheard Trent talking to his baby boy in the high-chair.

"Jimmy made a great choice. They are going to be happy, Benny, very happy."

Hearing their one-sided conversation put a big smile on Kelsey's face.

A few hours later the Kelly's living room was transformed into a lovely white wedding scene. A beautiful arch decorated with flowers graced one wall. White chairs set in rows of five had been set up on each side of the room. A white cloth runner adorned the middle of those chairs which led to the wedding arch. The back of the room was filled with three long tables set with white linen tablecloths, candles and fresh flowers on each one. To

Kelsey it didn't look anything like a living room any more, it now looked just like a sweet wedding chapel. That thought made her beam with happiness.

Kelsey's arms were full of fresh flowers when she caught sight of Trent watching his wife giving orders to the florist, with their baby on her hip. She knew by the look on his face he loved Candy and their life together. She hoped she and Jimmy would enjoy the same feeling as time when on.

All the women were down the hall when Jimmy, Bobby and Benet walked in the back door. Jimmy saw Trent smile over at them as he said, "So, I guess you haven't changed your mind, Jimmy."

"Can't, her hooks are in me too deep," he joked.

"Bullshit. I can see you love her, so don't act as though Kelsey reeled you in." Bobby blurted out as he slapped his back.

"Hell, you've been sniffin around her like an old hound dog ever since she first started working for us." Benet jumped into the conversation with both feet.

"Yeah, I guess I deserve that because I wasn't able to keep my eyes off her, and it was me who couldn't stop hounding her. Although, I also have to say, I don't regret one minute of it. She's definitely the girl for me." Jimmy nodded.

"Hey guys, the drinks are on Jimmy, bar's open!" Trent announced.

While the guys shared drinks in the kitchen, Candy walked into Torrie's room. She sighed at the sight before her, because Kelsey was such a pretty little thing, beautiful really. She wore a short little dress of white sparkling velvet; it was fitted with long sleeves. The neckline was low, a brightly shining, floating, rhinestone solitaire stone hung around her neck, matching earrings dangling from her ears.

Candy thought she looked perfect, from the spiked frosted short hair on her head, to the white velvet high heels on her feet.

"Oh, Kelsey, you're going to stop Jimmy's heart," Candy said.

A moment later she watched the bride smooth her dress down.

"I sure hope so." Kelsey giggled out.

"The minister has arrived and the guys are in the kitchen," Candy informed her.

"Jimmy's here?" Kelsey's excitement showed on her face.

"Come on, Kelsey, you didn't really think he'd stand you up, did you?"

"No, Jimmy wouldn't do that to me."

"You're damn right he wouldn't," Candy insisted.

Suddenly Candy noticed her sister Emma step into the room, holding a big square box in her hands. She stretched her short arms out to Kelsey and handed her the box. "Jimmy says you need this."

Candy smiled as the bride took the box and quickly opened it with excitement. Her eyes flew open when she lifted a colorful tied bouquet of fresh flowers out of the box. Candy knew she'd never forget the look on Kelsey's face. She could only describe it as pure love for the man in her life.

So Candy said quickly, "Wait right here. I've got to get a picture of this."

When Candy stepped back into the room, there were nonstop camera flashes. She figured Kelsey thought she wouldn't see clearly for a week. However, Candy also knew Kelsey would cherish the pictures for life.

The guys were laughing and talking when they were surprised by Candy's camera. Every one of them cursed her but she paid them no mind. This occasion would be documented nicely whether they liked it or not.

It wasn't long before Candy was back with Kelsey, telling her it was time.

However, out in the living room the door opened and Bobby saw her. It was Torrie. He hurried over to her and took the bag out of her hand.

"I'm not late, am I?" she whispered.

"You mean for the wedding? No, what are you doing here?" Bobby asked softly.

"Candy called me yesterday and told me about Jimmy and Kelsey. Seeing I wasn't on duty until Wednesday, I decided to come home. I jumped on a train and here I am." She gave him a big smile.

"I'm so glad you did." And he gave her a hug and a wink which made her heart race. Yet she had to ask, "Where's Candy and Kelsey?"

"Your room," he said, and he led the way, carrying her bag for her.

Once he closed the bedroom door, he took a deep breath. The sight of Torrie always made his heart pound a wild beat. He leaned against the doorjamb, his arms folded across his chest. Damn, what was he going to do about this feeling he had for Torrie? He wanted to just say the hell with being mister goodie, goodie, and being all understanding about her dreams and what she wants and needs. What about him? What about what Bobby wants, what he needs?

He took another deep breath; maybe he'd get her in a dark corner and kiss her like he really wanted to kiss her. Hold her in his arms, caress her body, smell her hair. Throw her over his shoulder and carry her off and make mad passionate love to her. He sighed.

Oh, damn it to hell, you're not going to do any of that. You're going to steal a kiss and a hug when you can and try to forget about what you want. He kicked the carpet under his feet and walked away.

The guys were all in front of the flower covered arch when Bobby watched Torrie enter the room. He felt his heart beat wildly again. She was wearing a sapphire blue full skirted dress. Her long frosted blonde hair lay over her shoulders and down her back, black glitter flip flops on her feet.

All Bobby did was smile and shake his head at her choice of shoes. How he wished it was his wedding day and Torrie was the bride. Damn, no matter how he tried, he just couldn't get her out of his blood.

Kelsey was still down the hall when Candy came rushing out, the baby in her arms.

"Now, Tess," she whispered loudly, and her little sister went to the stereo and pushed a button and everyone heard a beautiful classical song began to play. The baby was handed to Torrie and in a slow hesitated step Candy approached the arch and the minister.

Kelsey slipped out into the living room once Candy stood next to the minister and Jimmy's breath got caught in his throat. She knew he'd never seen her looking like this. She sure wished the expression on his face meant he really did love her or at least thought she was pretty.

Kelsey flashed him a beautiful smile as she slowly approached him. She hoped he knew he was marrying the perfect woman for him because at this moment she was sure she was marrying the perfect man for her.

When she stood next to him he took hold of her hand and they both turned to the Minister where they promised to love and honor one another until death do they part.

Once they were pronounced husband and wife there was applause from their friends and Jimmy took Kelsey into his arms and placed a passionate kiss on her lips.

Even though they didn't have a big wedding, they were pleased with who was there; thirty people attended in all, the Big 4 family and a few good people they'd met along the way. It was just perfect.

The couple had a wonderful wedding day with their friends. There were gifts, wonderful food, and plenty of conversation and laughs.

Amazingly, Kelsey and Jimmy stood by while Torrie caught the bouquet. Strangely enough, Bobby caught the garter out of mid air. The newlyweds watched as Bobby and Torrie shared a provocative little dance. And when it was over, Bobby placed the garter on Torrie's thigh. Everyone hooted and hollered as he slid it easily up her shapely leg.

It was dark, but the celebration was still going on when the bride and groom left Trent and Candy's house. Laughter grabbed hold of the couple as they were barraged by flying white grains of rice all the way to Jimmy's truck.

It wasn't long before Jimmy led her into a lovely hotel lobby. Her new husband went after the key while she stood in the middle of the floor. He couldn't help but watch with delight as his new wife smiled at one person after another, who congratulated her. He thought she looked every inch the beautiful bride, because she sure was.

Jimmy was dangling the key at her when he took hold of her hand. A moment later they were alone in the elevator and he pushed her up against the back wall where he planted an erotic kiss on her lips. His tongue plundered her mouth over and over again, and his hands took hold of her butt and pulled her closer. He didn't stop his hot advances until the elevator doors opened again.

Once out of the elevator Jimmy looked lovingly into her eyes, and with one more kiss he walked her to their room and unlocked the door. They stepped in and he locked it behind them.

He was giving her a devilish smile when she backed away from him. "You're mine, Kelsey. You can't get away from me now."

He shrugged out of his tuxedo jacket and threw it on the back of a chair. Then he pulled off his shoes, one at a time, then approached his new wife. He slowly began unbuttoning his shirt and she was still backing away.

"Jimmy, we're barely in the door, don't you want to go slow?"

"Not particularly." The smile he gave her was completely despicable and full of the devil. It all made her feel awfully nervous all of a sudden.

Jimmy caught her expression and he knew he needed to slow down for her. He stopped and rubbed his chin thoughtfully. Kelsey had been through a lot. Her brother's attack on her was only two days ago. It had only been that long since he'd asked her to marry him. There hadn't been any time to even tell her how he felt about her. He had to remind himself, she was now his wife and she wasn't Tina. Again he smiled, because he was sure glad she wasn't.

Then he noticed the questioning look on her face so he walked over to a chair next to the bed and slowly sat down. He cricked his finger at her, motioning her over to him. Her fingers were pulling on her skirt as she approached.

Jimmy was holding back the laughter when he looked up at her. His wife truly looked as if she wanted to run for the hills. Yet he kept his expression calm and cool when he said, "Come here, sit with me." He patted his thigh as he spoke.

He sat waiting until Kelsey slid into his lap. Almost instantly he realized she was trying not to look into his eyes. She probably didn't want him to see how nervous she was. A lot had happened since they were going to make love two nights ago. He just wanted her to know how he felt about her.

Jimmy started off by placing his hand on the back of her head and the other on her cheek at the same time. He now had her full attention. Smiling softly, he said, "Things kind of got away from us the last two days, didn't they?"

He saw her nod slowly. She was still nervous. he could feel it in the tightness of her body. So he wrapped his arms around her and drew her close.

"Things didn't go as I'd planned on Valentines Day. The call from Trent that pulled me away from you, Josh coming after you, trying to kill you. The guys and Candy taking over the wedding, No, it didn't go at all like I planned."

"It was a beautiful little wedding though, don't you think?"

"Kelsey, I'll never forget our wedding and the way you looked. God, I wanted to take you in my arms right there in front of the minister." He grinned when Kelsey giggled.

"Thank God you didn't." She placed her hands over her mouth to cover up the laughter.

He rewarded her giggle with a handsome smile.

"I did mean to tell you something, something really important. It's been on my mind for a long while now," he said.

"What is it?" Her expression seemed quite serious.

Jimmy slid his fingers gently over her lips. "I love you, Kelsey, you're the girl for me. Seems I've known that from the beginning. But, me being the man I am, I tried to push it away. I tried to give it another name and when I think back, it happened when you first climbed up on the big rig engine with me.

Remember when you rolled under the truck and placed those headphones on my head and your sexy little body rubbed against mine? Oh man, my body screamed at me to reevaluate all the other girls in my life. All I wanted to do was see you clearly, and Lord, am I glad I did, because suddenly I understood I loved you. So even though you said yes to my proposal and married me, I have to ask, "Do you love me enough to stay at my side until I leave this earth?"

Jimmy saw her give him a brilliant smile, as she placed her arms around his neck and said, "Forever, Jimmy, forever."

He was staring into her eyes as he pulled her close enough to feel her breasts snug up against his wide chest. He could feel her heart pounding nearly as frantically as his was. Although he didn't kiss her right away, just sat there staring into her eyes. There seemed to be questions and passion in those sparkling eyes of hers. Questions about him that would all be answered tonight and the smile on his face grew large.

"What?" she couldn't help but ask.

He didn't answer her question, at least not in words. His mouth took total possession of not only her lips, but her soul, slanting over hers again and again, which made Kelsey pull herself even closer to Jimmy's body. She wanted everything he was offering, even more. Especially now, because she knew how he felt about her.

At that moment he slid his hand up over her stockinged thigh to the garter belt that held them, and when he ventured further, he felt the bare cheeks of her beautifully smooth butt. She was wearing a thong and the thought of it made him moan into her mouth.

Jimmy saw Kelsey pulling her coat off—he hoped it was in an effort to feel his body against hers. She barely got her coat off when Jimmy pulled her dress over her head, revealing a very low cut white lace bra and thong, garter belt and stockings, God, she looked absolutely delicious. He just wanted to taste her all over.

He scanned every inch of her body until their eyes met once more.

"Well, Jimmy, do you approve, or do I have to get an annulment?" She could see her comment had taken him back.

"Hell yeah, I approve!"

He caught her off guard when he placed his finger on the tip of her nose. "There'll be no way out of this marriage, Kelsey, and if I ever hear you mention anything like that again, you'll be feelin my hand on your pretty little bottom. And although, right now the idea of sliding my fingers slowly over those soft cheeks of your sexy little butt, I'll hold back my desire to make em 'red for you." He said seriously.

Kelsey swallowed hard, not at just the thought of a spanking, but the seductive sound of her bottom being described to her. It made her mouth go dry. All she could do was nod to her husband in understanding.

The only warning she received of his intentions was the sparkle in his eyes when again, he devoured her lips. Kelsey thought he tasted delicious, sweet and salty all at the same time. And the feeling of his hand rubbing her thighs and bottom gave her a hot sensation she'd never experienced from anyone before.

While she was thinking of how her body was reacting, her bra was being unhooked and pulled off. The next thing she knew, he was kissing the valley between her breasts at the same time he was unfastening her stockings. God she wanted to help him. She couldn't shed her confinements fast enough. Kelsey wanted to help but he wouldn't let her because what he was doing to her chest had her full attention now.

The only thing left on her body was her lovely white lace thong. When he took her erect nipple into his mouth, she never even felt him slide her thong off. All she could think of was where he was taking her, which was to passion, and she went willingly.

When he took her other nipple into his warm mouth, he lifted her up and into his arms and carried her to the bed where he pulled back the covers and laid her down.

Kelsey was stark naked laying in the middle of the bed. She was clutching the bottom sheet, each arm stretched out to it's full length. She remembered thinking she should be cold but she also knew the passion in Jimmy's eyes was what was keeping her warm.

She was being held captive by the sparkle in his eyes. They were warm, loving even until she saw him pull his open shirt off and Kelsey inspected every inch of his chest. A moment later his socks were thrown down. Yet, when he unbuckled his trousers, the anticipation made her swallow hard. Although, it was the sight of his large hardness that made her almost swallow her tongue because he gave her plenty of time to take a good long look at what he had to offer.

Their eyes locked when he came over her, resting most of his weight on his elbows. Kelsey watched him stare straight into her eyes and whisper, "As you can see by the look of me, I'm aching for you, but I promise to go slow and not rush this." His voice sounded gruff.

She just nodded and he gave her a wink. Right there and then she knew he would take complete control and he started with a luscious kiss, one that had her in his power and he didn't stop there. Before she knew it he was placing hot kisses down her throat, down her breasts where he seared his mouth to her nipples once again.

Kelsey thought for sure she would lose all control, shatter in a million pieces. Although what happened next made her want to scream. Jimmy placed those hot kisses on the soft curls of what her mother used to call, her powder puff. And when he slid his fingers into her sleek folds, she couldn't help but gasp, "Oh Jimmy."

There was only one light on in the room and it was in the living room area, although somehow she knew when he looked up at her, he was smiling. Then he eased himself slowly inside her.

Immediately she could feel how wonderful he felt deep inside her. She couldn't believe it was her voice begging him to go deeper. Yes, it was her voice, her pleas. Not only was she screaming it, her body was also screaming with every movement. She kept pulling him closer, the way her hips instinctively moved against his made her crazy. Lord, there was no other word for it. Yes, crazy, said it all!

Suddenly waves of climax devoured her. She didn't know how to handle the sweet torture. All she knew was she wanted him, harder and deeper. Kelsey couldn't get enough. She knew her body language spoke to Jimmy because he whispered in a rough, ragged voice she hardly recognized.

"Wrap your legs around my waist."

She did exactly as he said and moaned when he came fully into her. The mating ritual as old as time itself took them both to a place where only the two of them could share, where they could soar together into pure fiery pleasure.

Kelsey was deep in her own depths of passion when Jimmy filled her with his seed and she quivered with it. She was trying to understand her feelings when Jimmy rolled over on the bed, bringing her with him. They were both still breathing hard when they lay entwined in each other's arms.

Oh, sweet thing, I have to tell you. Not only does your body scream touch me, your passion drove me past my own endurance." He chuckled as he rubbed her smooth butt.

She thought his soft, warm chuckle was very sexy.

"Did I hurt you?" he asked as he touched the curve of her cheek. "Was I too rough? Because you drove me wild, it was as though I lost all control."

"No, it was wonderful and…" She smiled at him, "all consuming."

"So, I satisfied you?"

She rolled over on top of him, and kissed him with all the passion she could give. And as she pulled away, she said, "You did more than satisfy, Jimmy." He wrapped his arms around her as she continued, "You made me feel things I never felt before. Yes, husband, I was satisfactorily made love to." She nodded her head for emphasis.

Kelsey giggled when Jimmy rolled her onto her back and he whispered, "Yes, you were made love to by your very own husband." And he covered her mouth with his all over again until they were making hot passionate love once more.

17

Kelsey and Jimmy hadn't left their honeymoon suite in two days, except to eat. They had just gotten out of the shower together. He was drying his wife off intimately, when the phone rang.

"Don't move a muscle, Kelsey, I'll be right back." Jimmy wrapped a towel around his waist as he left the bathroom.

Kelsey wrapped a towel around her and stared out the large round window overlooking Lake Huron. She smiled as she thought of the last two days of her honeymoon. It was full of fine living and love making. The memory of last night's dinner made her sigh. Her husband took her to a lovely restaurant downstairs where she ate only her second lobster and where they danced together. She rubbed her upper arms as she remembered how he held her. The night ended in love making. Yes, they'd made love three times last night. God, she loved her husband, how did she live all this time without him?

Then her thoughts went to her brother Josh. She was praying he was firmly tucked away in jail where she would never have to lay eyes on him again. Kelsey hated her brother for not only taking everything from her, but also for never letting her have a life.

That's when she realized if it hadn't been for Josh, she would never have run to Port Austin. Never would have met her handsome husband, nor would she be a happily married woman right now. Yes, she guessed Josh did deserve his due, but damn, she wouldn't give the man anything else.

A moment later Kelsey's husband's arms were around her waist. His lips placed butterfly kisses on her neck and shoulders, she couldn't help but sigh.

She reached up and slid her fingers through his hair. "I love you, Jimmy," she whispered.

"I love you too, just remember that, because I have to go."

She turned around to face him. "Go where?"

"The call was from Bobby. Seems Trent's truck won't start, and it's got a full load on it, which has to be in Ohio by 6 a.m., so I've got to go," he explained.

She gave him a big smile. "So, I'll go with you."

"Oh, no you won't. I have to concentrate, and if you're there I'll be thinking only about one thing."

She placed her hands on her hips. "And what's that?"

"Throwing you in the cab of the truck and... Well, I'm sure if you let your imagination take over, you can figure it out!" He chuckled.

Kelsey wrapped her arms around his waist and looked up at him with a sexy little grin. "Okay, Jimmy, how are we going to work together?"

"I'm hoping at the end of these next two weeks you'll have worn me out enough to get through a day of work." He gave her butt a love slap. "I got to go."

Kelsey watched Jimmy head for the bathroom door when she shouted, "What am I supposed to do while you're gone?"

"Order room service, eat and rest, because you're gonna need it when I get back." He watched her swallow hard and he couldn't help, but laugh out loud.

Later, Kelsey was dressed and spiking her short hair when the doorbell rang. She hurried to the door and looked out the peep hole. "Who is it?"

"Room service." She saw only the cart and thought immediately, Jimmy had ordered her food.

At the exact time she opened the door, the phone rang. So her attention was switched from the door to the phone.

"Excuse me," Kelsey said as she lifted the phone and said, "Jimmy, miss me already?"

The giggle stilled in her throat when she turned and saw a pistol in her face. The phone was still in her hand when she stepped back. Then she heard on the phone, "Hey Kelsey, the question is, do ya miss me?"

"Yeah, but not Josh," she said with a serious voice.

"What does that have to do with this?" Jimmy was taken back by her comment.

She answered him back in the same tone, "Everything."

Kelsey no sooner said the last word, she realized the person holding the pistol in her face was Tina, who whispered, "Get rid of him, now!"

So Kelsey said very quickly, "I got to go, bye," and she hung up the phone, and faced Tina.

"What are you doing, Tina? The Police don't even know you had a role in all of this, even Josh isn't a snitch."

"You don't get it, do you? This isn't about my little conspiracy with Josh, it's about you. I guess it's always has been, It's simple You're not having Jimmy. he's mine."

"You can't stop this, Tina, we're married, we've made love, we love each other," Kelsey admitted.

A moment later it was too late to reason with her because Kelsey didn't even have time to duck when Tina reached out and slapped her. All she could do was stagger back from the impact.

Kelsey grabbed hold of her cheek while she tried to calm the pain.

"You and Jimmy are through and once you're dead, your body dumped in the lake, he'll get over you. And when he does, you know who'll be the one to comfort him, don't you? Me… so you see it's quite simple, I get rid of you and reclaim my life and Jimmy too," Tina blurted out.

Kelsey shook her head slowly when Tina motioned the pistol to the door. "Get going and if you say a word to anyone, I'll kill you on the spot."

Kelsey stood tall, all 5 foot 4 of her as she said, "What do I care? You're gonna shoot me anyway."

"Because if you don't do as I say, I have already found a guy who will kill every last one of the Big 4 truckers, including Jimmy if I'm found out."

She could gamble with her life but not with her bosses' lives, especially not with Jimmy's. So she did as she was told.

Kelsey knew Tina had the pistol in her pocket and it was pointed right at her. She didn't have to see the gun because Tina would poke it into her back every now and again to remind her. It only made her think of what was going to happen next.

The two women walked across the grass and into the woods, which was adjacent to the lake. Kelsey figured this was the place where she was going to die.

Once inside the green cover of the forest, Tina pulled the pistol out of her coat.

"Keep walking." Tina insisted.

Kelsey did exactly what she was told until she saw the ice and the waves of the lake slapping up against the shoreline. The wind howled and whipped at her body. There was no coat to shield her from the frigid gusts off the water and now she was shaking with the cold.

She stilled at the sight of the place of her death because Kelsey felt the barrel of the gun pushed into the small of her back once more.

"Move it, now!" Tina pushed her.

Kelsey tripped on a thick tree root and Tina caught her.

"We wouldn't want anything to happen to you and have my pleasure taken away from me, now would we?" Tina threatened.

Kelsey stumbled to her feet with only an angry look back at Tina. All the stupid cow did was laugh. Lord, there was no doubt, Tina was a mad woman.

Moments later, Kelsey stood on the shoreline of Lake Huron, while Tina backed away from her.

"Turn around. I want you to see this coming," Tina snapped.

Kelsey turned and saw the pistol pointed at her. At the same time she suffered a surge of icy cold water splash against her shoes. She wanted to scream and find somewhere warm to hide, but it wasn't possible.

So she closed her eyes, praying her death wouldn't be painful. In that instant her thoughts turned to Jimmy and how much she loved him; she really did want to grow old with him.

"Take a look around, cause it's your last." The sound of Tina's demented voice had her full attention once more.

"Think this over, Tina, if you kill me the police will figure you did it." Kelsey tried to reason with her.

"It doesn't matter, because right now I have a man friend who is willing to say I was with him all day. It's amazing what you can do with money." She seemed to almost growl it out.

"I thought Josh took every penny of your money?" Kelsey couldn't believe it.

"Josh told you that, didn't he? The man believed exactly what I wanted him to. I knew if he thought I had money he would have taken every penny he could. So, I acted as if I were upset, as if I didn't have any money left, and the stupid fool believed me. But enough of this. It's time for you to meet your maker." Tina's laugh sounded sinister.

Kelsey could hear the click of the hammer of Tina's pistol as she pulled it back from where she stood. It seemed to echo in her ears. She even swore she heard the trigger being pulled back. Her eyes were wide open when Kelsey saw it happen.

Out of nowhere, Jimmy appeared. He had come up behind Tina and slammed his fist into her shoulder and she went down. However, he was too late. Tina had already fired her gun and he watched Kelsey collapse to her knees in front of his eyes.

Jimmy lifted the pistol from the ground on his way to his wife, leaving Tina crying in pain. Not even a moment had passed when he was kneeling on the shore next to his wife, scanning every inch of her body. He only saw one wound. The bullet went clear through the fleshy part of her arm.

Jimmy didn't say a word to his wife. He was too overwhelmed by the whole experience. The lump in his throat was large, so much so he couldn't seem to speak. So silently he went right to work. He tugged the end of his shirt off and tied it tightly around her arm to slow down the bleeding.

That's when the police found them.

Jimmy answered all their questions as he tended to his wife's wound. Through the whole thing, Kelsey just kept staring into the worried eyes of her husband.

He looked up at Tina as she shouted for him to help her. All he could do was shake his head at her pleas for help. He decided she was a very disturbed woman. He was now thanking his lucky stars that he'd ended their relationship and that he'd found Kelsey.

He turned away from Tina's shouts and saw Kelsey being placed on a litter by the EMS. Jimmy followed behind her until they we're out of the woods, then he went to her side and took hold of her good hand. He saw she was looking up at him with love.

"How can you look at me like that? Especially after what my ex-girlfriend did to you?" Jimmy shook his head.

"You're being ridiculous, You saved my life, you're my hero. So, you understood my hint on the phone?" Kelsey smiled at the pain in his eyes.

"I have to admit it took me a while. It didn't hit me until I was on my way back here to you. I called the police to see where Josh was. The guy was still in the hospital, under guard. A moment later it occurred to me, maybe it was Billy, only to immediately forget the notion. I remembered the look in his eyes as he spoke to you, no matter what the guy did, he loved his sister. So, the only one left in this whole mess was, Tina. Although, I have to say, I didn't want to admit Tina could do such a thing. I always knew she was possessive, but this crazy, I didn't have a clue!"

"How did you know I was out here? she asked.

Jimmy took a deep breath. "I didn't at first. I went to our room and the cleaning lady said you left with another woman. She pointed out the window at the woods and said she saw you two go in, even pointed out where you went in exactly. I told her to call the police and I hurried to you. Boy, am I glad she was a nosey maid, other wise I may not have found you in time."

"It's alright, Jimmy, it's all over." She squeezed his hand.

Damn it, she was comforting him. "Hell, stop being so nice to me. This is all my fault you're on this litter and in pain too, damn it."

"None of this is your fault. It's Tina's, and you know what, I still love you." Her smile grew large.

They were about to put Kelsey in the ambulance when he leaned down and gently kissed her.

"I'll follow you—we'll talk later."

He stood watching as they put her inside the ambulance and he waved to her until the doors were closed.

18

A few days had gone by when Kelsey was driven home from the hospital by her husband, who arranged her on the couch of the third story flat. They had decided the flat had enough room for the both of them and Kelsey loved it there.

Her arm was propped up on two pillows, her foot on a footstool. Jimmy was sitting beside her when their door opened and the whole Big 4 family came rushing in. Trent, Candy, and their new baby were the first in the door, Bobby and Benet right behind.

Kelsey watched Candy push Jimmy up and she sat in his spot and Kelsey made silly noises at the baby.

"How are you, Kelsey?" Candy asked quite seriously.

"Don't worry about me, Candy, I'm doing fine. The doctor says I can go back to work in two weeks."

"If she continues to rest," Jimmy qualified. "I'm having a hell of a time keeping this girl down. She wants to continue doing everything around here. I'm beginning to think she'd get more rest at work."

"We sure do miss you, Kelsey, and can't wait for you to return. But, we're worried more about your health than we are about the damn work." Bobby took over the conversation.

"I sure do miss your sweet voice on the radio, beats the hell out of

Bobby's serious damn squawking!" Benet pushed his way into the conversation.

"What the hell are you talking about? I'm not serious, I'm always upbeat," Bobby defended.

"Suffice to say, we all miss you, you're part of our family now and when you're not there, you're missed," Trent said.

"Thanks, guys, I miss all of you, too." Kelsey smiled.

"Benet, I owe you an apology. You were right about Tina. Not only was she manipulating and jealous, she was also a real Hoochi Mama," Jimmy confessed.

"Forget about it. I guess I had a few women do the same thing to me. That's how I could spot it so easy on you," he leaned close to Jimmy and said so only he could hear.

"But you made up for it by marrying this little Sweetheart here. Make sure you hold her close because someone like Kelsey doesn't come but once in a lifetime," Benet said as he slapped him on the back.

"I will remember," Jimmy said as he looked into Benet's eyes with conviction.

Six weeks later Big 4 was back on the road again. Kelsey was back in the office and on the radio. And Jimmy was back to fixing their trucks.

Everyone stood around drinking coffee when Kelsey got a call from a parts warehouse so she went into the garage. Jimmy was under a truck so she grabbed another creeper, rolled under it and placed the headphones on his ears. She lay there looking at the truck's muffler system when her headphones were placed back on her head.

Before she could even say a word, Jimmy pulled her on top of him. She took a deep breath when his hands grabbed hold of each cheek of her butt and he squeezed her closer to him.

"You know, Kelsey, I've always wanted to make love under a big rig, just like this." And he gave her an earth shattering kiss which took her a few moments to recover from.

"Not now, Jimmy, everyone's here." She looked all around.

"Who cares?" He shrugged it off.

"I care. They're my bosses. Do you want me to lose my job?"

"I'm a boss too. Don't you have to do what I say?" He thought he had her.

She thought for a moment and smiled. "Nope!"

"What do you mean, no?"

"Remember, you told me you wouldn't be my boss if I'd date you? So no, I don't have to listen to you." She nodded for emphasis.

"I lied!" Jimmy couldn't help but laugh at the expression on her face. A moment later she rolled over onto her creeper and slid out from under the truck. She could still hear the laughter as she straightened up and went back inside the office.

Kelsey went right to the coffee pot and poured herself a cup. She was trying to calm down. Not only was she trying to put his kiss out of her mind, but damn him, she kept telling herself, he couldn't do what he said he could under the truck, not in broad daylight with his partners right here, or would he? Suddenly she heard the laughter.

She turned on her bosses. "What's so funny?"

"You are. Did you see the seat of your slacks?" Bobby asked.

She stretched her neck to see what they were talking about as the guys continued to laugh.

"They're laughing at my hand prints on your ass, my brand," Jimmy explained. She turned the darkest red and now he joined in the laughter.

Kelsey grabbed her purse and headed for the door, but she didn't get far. Jimmy grabbed hold of her arm and pulled her up against him. His hands were back on her butt again and he pulled her real close to him and gave her a luscious kiss.

"Looks like the handprints on Kelsey's ass fit Jimmy's hands perfectly," Bobby said to his partners.

Yep, he's guilty!" Benet said with a chuckle.

"Now, fun's fun, but everyone back to work. Jimmy, you've got trucks to fix. Kelsey, Benet's going on the road and so am I, so dispatch us. And Bobby don't you have some contracts to sell?" Trent announced.

Kelsey saw the guys go in three different directions and Trent smiled.

"What are you smiling at, Trent?"

"You, because you've become a great part of Big 4. I also think you won't have any trouble keeping the kid in line. And with that being said, I'm off Kelsey. I'll check in at the half way mark. Oh, and have I told you welcome back?"

She shook her head at him.

"Well, we're happy to have our Kelsey back. You fit us all nearly as well as Jimmy's hands fit your backside." He watched her turn red and walked right out the door laughing.

Once the office was quiet again, Kelsey smiled. Her husband and his partners were sure a handful, but lord, how she loved Jimmy and their Big 4 family. Yes, Kelsey had finally found her place and it was right here with Jimmy and Big 4. Then the switchboard lit up and she pressed a button, "Big 4 trucking, can I help you?"

Watch for *Big 4 Trucking* #3, and find out if Bobby and Torrie are going to finally find each other, or could there be someone else in their future? Shift into third gear and find out!

Big 4 Trucking #3
Worth Waiting For

THANK YOU FOR READING

Did you enjoy this book?

We invite you to leave a review at your favorite book site, such as Goodreads, Amazon, Barnes & Noble, etc.

DID YOU KNOW THAT LEAVING A REVIEW…

- Helps other readers find books they may enjoy.
- Gives you a chance to let your voice be heard.
- Gives authors recognition for their hard work.
- Doesn't have to be long. A sentence or two about why you liked the book will do.

Don't miss out on your next favorite book!

Join the Satin Romance mailing list
www.satinromance.com/mail.html

Subscriber Perks Include:

- First peeks at upcoming releases.
- Exclusive giveaways.
- News of book sales and freebies right in your inbox.
- And more!

ABOUT THE AUTHOR

Victoria Staat has been writing for almost fifteen years. She always wanted to write, but sometimes life takes the front seat and you get the back. Yet that didn't stop her from diving in and working hard.

She lives in Warren Michigan and has been married to her husband John for forty-three years. The years have blessed her with a son John and a daughter Angie, and now a lovely granddaughter; Madison.

When Victoria isn't writing, she's in the kitchen cooking, or baking. Old time rock and roll, classic cars, squirt gun fights, and enjoying their cottage in Port Austin Michigan, are among her favorite things to do.

Now she starts a new chapter in her life. Because she's proud and excited to be joining forces with Melange Publishing on her newest book; *My Kind of Fashion Model.*

victoriastaat.vpweb.com
facebook.com/Victoria-Staat-1506233202967466
facebook.com/The-Sixties-Girl-297501127127454
facebook.com/vicky.staat
twitter.com/VictoriaStaat
plus.google.com/u/0/+VictoriaStaat

ALSO BY VICTORIA STAAT

Big 4 Trucking
Eye Candy
My Kind of Fashion Model
Worth Waiting For (Spring 2018)
Behind The Screen Door (Spring/Summer 2018)